"Don't overdramatize, Jean-Luc," Q said.

"Perhaps I was a trifle blind, in an omniscient sort of way, but ultimately it was a mere prank, nothing more. A trifle mean-spirited, I concede, but there was no real harm done, not permanently. In the grand cosmic scheme of things, the Calamarain were merely inconvenienced, not actually injured in any way that need concern us here."

"That's all you have to say about it?" Picard demanded, offended by Q's cavalier tone. "An entire species frozen into suspended animation for heaven knows how long. . . ."

Q shrugged his shoulders. "Can I help it if the Calamarain didn't see the funny side of it?"

"If what I witnessed just now was nothing more than a prank," Picard declared indignantly, "then I shudder to think what you would consider genuine maliciousness."

Q gave Picard a smile that chilled the captain's blood. "You should. . . ."

STAR TREK
THE NEXT GENERATION®

THE Q CONTINUUM

BOOK TWO OF THREE

Q-ZONE

GREG COX

POCKET BOOKS
New York   London   Toronto   Sydney   Tokyo   Singapore

An *Original* Publication of POCKET BOOKS

POCKET BOOKS, a division of Simon & Schuster Inc.
1230 Avenue of the Americas, New York, NY 10020

Copyright © 1998 by Paramount Pictures. All Rights Reserved.

STAR TREK is a Registered Trademark of Paramount Pictures.

A VIACOM COMPANY

This book is published by Pocket Books, a division of Simon & Schuster Inc., under exclusive license from Paramount Pictures.

ISBN: 0-671-01921-X

First Pocket Books printing August 1998

10 9 8 7 6 5 4 3 2 1

Printed in the U.S.A.

Q-ZONE

Prologue

SOON, HE CACKLED. SOONER. SOONEST.

Behind the wall, he watched with keen anticipation as lesser life-forms, no more than a bug or a wisp of smoke to him, buzzed about on the other side. Only the wall, the wretched wall that had kept him out for longer than his muddled memory could even begin to encompass, kept him from reaching forth and swatting both bug and smoke away. Tendrils of his contorted consciousness capered spiderlike against the edge of the wall, scraping away at the boundaries of his banishment. He couldn't touch the other side just yet, but he could watch and wait and wonder about what he would do when the wall, the wicked and wearying wall, finally came down.

Very soon, he singsonged, *soon soon soon*. The

wall would crumble. The voice had promised him so, that teensy-tiny voice from the other side. It was difficult to conceive how such a paltry piece of protoplasm could possibly undo that which had held him back for so long, but he had hope and reason to believe. Already he sensed that the wall was weaker than before, minute faults and fissures undermining its primal, protracted permanence. All it needed was one good push from the other side and a gap would be formed, the gap he needed to break through. *And then . . . and then what time has done to the galaxy will be nothing compared to what I'll do to all those stars and planets and people.* He flexed his tendrils in his eagerness to be free once more. *Yes, that's right, all the things I'll do . . . to Q and Q and Q.*

There was only one thing that worried him. What if someone silenced the other voice before it fulfilled its promise? And not just anyone someone, but Q. That Q, the quisling Q, the Q who could never, ever be trusted. *I can smell you, Q.* His stench was all over the shiny silver bug on the other side. It stank and perhaps could sting. *Stink, stank, sting, bee,* he chanted to himself. *You can't stop me. Q can't escape me.*

Soon could not come soon enough. . . .

Chapter One

Ship's log, stardate 500146.3, First Officer William T. Riker reporting.

Captain Picard is missing, abducted by the capricious entity known as Q. We can only pray that Q will return the captain unharmed, although time has taught us that Q is nothing if not unpredictable.

The captain's disappearance cannot have come at a worse time, as the Enterprise *is under attack by the gaseous life-forms whom Q calls the Calamarain. Although Lieutenant Commander Data has succeeded in adapting our Universal Translator to the Calamarain's inhuman language, allowing us a degree of communication with them, we have thus far failed to win their trust. They have rendered our warp engines inactive and will not permit us to retreat, so we must persuade them otherwise. Speed is imperative, as our time is running out.*

To complicate matters, we have a number of potentially disruptive guests aboard the ship. Chief among them are a mysterious woman and boy who claim to be Q's mate and child. Like Q himself, these individuals treat the ship and its crew as mere toys for their amusement. Furthermore, they appear unwilling or unable to inform us where Q has taken Captain Picard.

Equally uncooperative is Professor Lem Faal, a distinguished Betazoid physicist, whose ambitious attempt to breach the immense energy barrier surrounding our galaxy has been interrupted by the unexpected arrivals of both the Q family and the Calamarain. Dying of an incurable disease, and obsessed with completing his work in the time remaining to him, Faal has vigorously challenged my decision to abort the experiment in light of the unanticipated dangers we now face. While I sympathize with the man's plight, I cannot allow his single-minded determination to endanger the ship further.

Indeed, according to what we have gathered from the Calamarain, our first effort to dare the barrier was the very event that provoked

*the Calamarain's wrath, thus threatening us
all with destruction. . . .*

THE STORM RAGED AROUND THEM. From the bridge of
the *Enterprise-E,* Commander William Riker could
see the fury of the Calamarain on the forward
viewscreen. The massive plasma cloud that comprised the foe, and that now enclosed the entire
Sovereign-class starship, had grown increasingly
turbulent over the last few hours. The sentient,
ionized gases outside the ship churned and billowed upon the screen; it was like being trapped in
the center of the galaxy's biggest thunderhead.
Huge sonic explosions literally shook the floor
beneath his feet, while brilliant arcs of electrical
energy flashed throughout the roiling cloud, inter-
secting violently with their own diminished
shields. The distinctive blue flare of Cerenkov
radiation discharged whenever the shield repelled
another bolt of lightning from the Calamarain,
which was happening far too often for Riker's
peace of mind.

With the captain absent, his present where-
abouts unknown, Riker was in command, and fighting a losing battle against alien entities determined
to destroy them. *Not this time,* he vowed silently,
determined not to lose another *Enterprise* while
Jean-Luc Picard was away. Once, in that cataclysmic crash into Veridian III, was enough for one
lifetime. *Never again,* he thought, remembering the

5

sick sensation he had felt when that grand old ship had slammed into its final port. *Not on my watch.*

Their present circumstances were precarious, though. Warp engines down, shields fading, and no sign yet that the Calamarain were willing to abandon their ferocious attack on the ship, despite his sincere offer to abandon the experiment and retreat from the galactic barrier—on impulse if necessary. Diplomacy was proving as useless as their phasers, even though Riker remained convinced that this entire conflict was based solely on suspicion and misunderstanding. *Nothing's more tragic than a senseless battle,* he thought.

"Shields down to twenty percent," Lieutenant Baeta Leyoro reported. The Angosian security chief was getting a real baptism by fire on her first mission aboard the *Enterprise.* So far she had performed superlatively, even if Riker still occasionally expected to see Worf at the tactical station. "For a glorified blast of bad breath, they pack a hell of a punch."

Riker tapped his combadge to initiate a link to Geordi in Engineering. "Mr. La Forge," he barked, "we need to reinforce our shields, pronto."

Geordi La Forge's voice responded immediately. "We're doing what we can, Commander, but this tachyon barrage just keeps increasing in intensity." Riker could hear the frustration in the chief engineer's voice; Geordi had been working nonstop for hours. "It's eaten up most of our power to keep the ship intact this long. I've still got a few more tricks I can try, but we can't hold out indefinitely."

"Understood," Riker acknowledged, scratching his beard as he hastily considered the problem. The thunder and lightning of the storm, as spectacular as they looked and sounded, were only the most visible manifestations of the Calamarain's untempered wrath. The real danger was the tachyon emissions that the cloud creatures were somehow able to generate and direct against the *Enterprise*. Ironically, it was precisely those faster-than-light particles that prevented the ship from achieving warp speed. "What about adjusting the field harmonics?" he asked Geordi, searching for some way to shore up their defenses. "That worked before."

"Yeah," Geordi agreed, "but the Calamarain seem to have learned how to compensate for that. At best it can only buy us a little more time."

"I'll take whatever I can get," Riker said grimly. Every moment the deflectors remained in place gave them one more chance to find a way out. "Go to it, Mr. La Forge. Riker out."

He sniffed the air, detecting the harsh odor of burned circuitry and melted plastic. A few systems had already been fried by the relentless force of the aliens' assault, although nothing the auxiliary backups hadn't been able to pick up. The Calamarain had drawn first blood nonetheless, while the starship crew's own phasers had done little more than anger the enraged cloud of plasma even further, much to the annoyance of Baeta Leyoro, who took the failure of their weapons personally.

This is all Q's fault, Riker thought. Captain Picard had shielded Q from the Calamarain several years ago, and apparently they had neither forgotten nor forgiven that decision. It was the *Enterprise*'s past association with Q, he believed, that made the Calamarain so unwilling to trust Riker now when he promised to abort Professor Faal's wormhole experiment. Tarred by Q's bad reputation . . . talk about adding insult to (possibly mortal) injury!

For all we know, he mused, *the Calamarain might have sound reasons for objecting to the experiment. If only they could be reasoned with somehow!* He glanced over at Counselor Deanna Troi, seated to his left at her own command station. "What are you picking up from our stormy friends out there?" he asked her. The seriousness in his eyes belied the flippancy of his words. "Any chance they might be calming down?"

Troi closed her eyes as she reached out with her empathic senses to probe the emotions of the seething vapors that had enveloped the ship. Her slender hands gently massaged her temples as her breathing slowed. No matter how many times Riker had seen Deanna employ her special sensitivity, it never failed to impress him. He prayed that Deanna would sense some room for compromise with the Calamarain. All he needed was to carve one chink in the other species' paranoia and he was sure he could find a peaceful solution to this needless conflict.

Blast you, Q, he thought bitterly. He had no idea what Q had done God-knows-when to infuriate the Calamarain so, but he was positive it was something stupid, infantile, and typically Q-like. *Why should he have treated them any differently than he's ever treated us?*

Riker's gaze swung inexorably to the right, where an imperious-looking auburn-haired woman rested comfortably in his own accustomed seat, a wide-eyed toddler bouncing on her knee while she observed the ongoing battle against the Calamarain with an air of refined boredom. Mother and child wore matching, if entirely unearned, Starfleet uniforms, with the woman bearing enough pips upon her collar to outrank Riker if they possessed any legitimacy—which they most definitely did not. The first officer shook his head quietly; he still found it hard to accept that this woman and her infant were actually Q's wife and son. Frankly, he had a rough time believing that any being, highly evolved or otherwise, would willingly enter into any sort of union with Q.

Then again, the female Q, if that's what she truly was, had enough regal attitude and ego to be one of Q's relations. *A match made in the Continuum,* he thought. She seemed content to treat the imminent annihilation of the ship and everyone aboard as no more important than a day at the zoo, which was probably just how she regarded the *Enterprise.* At least the little boy, whom she called q, appeared to be enjoying the show. He gaped wide-eyed at the screen, clapping his pudgy little hands at each spectacular display of pyrotechnics.

I'm glad somebody's having a good time, Riker thought ruefully. *I suppose I should be thankful that I don't have to worry about the kid's safety.* The two Qs were probably the only people aboard the *Enterprise* who weren't facing mortal danger. *Who knows?* he wondered. *They may even be at the heart of the problem.* Could the Calamarain tell that Q's family were on the ship? That couldn't possibly reflect well on the *Enterprise.*

"I'm sorry, Will," Troi said, reopening her eyes and lowering her hands to her lap. "All I can sense is anger and fear, just like before." She stared quizzically at the iridescent plasma surging across the viewer. "They're dreadfully afraid of us for some reason, and determined to stop us from interfering with the barrier."

The barrier, Riker thought. It all came back to the galactic barrier. He could no longer see the shimmering radiance of the barrier on the forward viewer, but he knew that the great, glowing curtain was only a fraction of a light-year away. For generations, ever since James Kirk first braved the galactic barrier in the original *Enterprise,* no vessel had ventured into it without suffering massive casualties and structural damage. Professor Faal had insisted that his wormhole experiment would have no harmful effect on the barrier as a whole, but the

Calamarain definitely seemed to feel otherwise. They referred to the barrier as the "moat" and had made it abundantly and forcefully clear that they would obliterate the *Enterprise* before they would permit the starship to tamper with it. *I need to find some way to convince them that we mean no harm.*

That might be easier accomplished without any Qs around to cloud the issue, he decided. "Excuse me," he said to the woman seated to his right ignoring for the moment the sound of the Calamarain pounding against the shields. He was unsure how to address her; although she claimed her name was Q as well, he still thought of her as *a* Q rather than *the* Q. "I'm afraid that the presence of you and your child upon the *Enterprise* may be provoking the Calamarain, complicating an already tense situation. As the acting commander of this vessel, I have to ask you to leave this ship immediately."

She peered down her nose at him as she might at a yapping dog whose pedigree left something to be desired. One eyebrow arched skeptically. For a second or two, Riker feared that she wasn't even going to acknowledge his request at all, but eventually she heaved a weary sigh. "Nonsense," she said, in a tone that reminded him rather too much of Lwaxana Troi at her most overbearing. "The Calamarain wouldn't dare threaten a Q. This is entirely between you and that noxious little species out there."

Riker rose from the captain's chair and looked

down on the seated woman, utilizing every possible psychological advantage at his disposal. She didn't look too impressed, and Riker recalled that, standing, the woman was nearly as tall as he was. "That may be so," he insisted, "but I can't afford to take that risk." He tried another tack. "Surely, in all the universe, there is someplace else you'd rather be."

"Several trillion," she informed him haughtily, "but dear q is amused by your little skirmish." She patted the boy's tousled head indulgently.

Don't think of her as godlike super-being, Riker thought as a new approach occurred to him. *Think of her as a doting mom.* His own mother had tragically died when he was very young, but Riker thought he understood the type. "Are you certain it's not too violent for him?" he asked, trying to sound as concerned and sympathetic as possible. "Things are likely to get messy soon, especially once our shields break down. It's not going to be pretty."

The woman's brow furrowed at his words. It appeared the potential grisliness of the crew's probable demise had not crossed her mind before. She glanced around her, checking out the various fragile humanoids populating the bridge. Outside, the tempest bellowed its intention to destroy the *Enterprise* and all aboard her. As if to make Riker's point, the ship pitched forward, slamming Lieutenant Leyoro into her tactical console. Her grunt of pain, followed by a look of stoic endurance, did not escape the female Q's notice.

Riker felt encouraged by her hesitant silence. *This might actually work,* he thought. "You know," he added, "I cried my eyes out the first time I read *Old Yeller.*"

The woman gave him a blank look; apparently her omniscience did not extend to classic children's fiction of the human species. Still, the basic idea seemed to get across. She cast a worried look at her son. "Perhaps you have a point," she conceded. Resignation settled onto her patrician features. "Too much mindless entertainment cannot be good for little q . . . even if his father can't get enough of your primitive antics."

With that, both mother and child vanished in a flash of white light that left Riker blinking. He breathed a sigh of relief, settling back into the captain's chair, until q reappeared upon his own knee. "Stay!" he yelped boisterously. For a superior being from a higher plane of reality, q felt solid enough and, if Riker could trust his own nostrils, in need of a fresh diaper beneath his miniature Starfleet uniform.

Riker groaned aloud. *Good thing the captain's still missing,* he thought, for the first and only time since Picard's abduction. The captain, it was well-known, had even less patience with small children than his first officer. *Now what do I do with this kid?* he wondered, looking rather desperately at Deanna for assistance. Despite their otherwise dire circumstances, the counselor could not resist a smile at Riker's sudden predicament.

Mercifully, the female Q materialized in front of Riker and lifted the toddler from his knee. "Come along, young q," she scolded gently. "I mean it." She tapped her foot impatiently upon the floor, giving Riker just enough warning to avert his eyes before the pair disappeared in another blinding flash of light.

He waited apprehensively for several seconds thereafter, holding his breath against the likelihood of another surprise reappearance. Had Q and q really left for the time being? He did not delude himself that the *Enterprise* had seen the last of either of them, let alone their mischievous relation, but he'd gladly settle for a temporary respite if it gave him enough time to settle matters with the Calamarain. *Just what we needed,* he thought sarcastically. *Three Qs to worry about from now on.*

Deanna broke the silence. "I think they're gone, Will."

"Thank heaven for small favors," he said. Now, if only the Calamarain could be disposed of so easily! "Mr. Data, activate your modified translation system. Now that our visitors have departed, let's try talking to the Calamarain one more time."

"Understood, Commander." The gold-skinned android manipulated the controls at Ops. After much effort, Data had devised a program by which humanoid language could be translated into the shortwave tachyon bursts the Calamarain used to communicate, and vice versa. "The translator is on-line. You may speak normally."

Riker leaned against the back of the captain's chair and took a deep breath. "This is Commander Riker of the *U.S.S. Enterprise,* addressing the Calamarain." In truth, he wasn't exactly sure whom he was speaking to. *Give me a face I can talk to any day,* he thought. "I'm asking you to call off your hostile actions toward our vessel. Speaking on behalf of this ship, and the United Federation of Planets, we are more than willing to discuss your concerns regarding the . . . moat. Let us return to our own space now, and perhaps our two peoples can communicate further in the future."

I can't get more direct than that, Riker thought. He could only hope that the Calamarain would realize how reasonable his offer was. *If not, our only remaining option may be to find a way to destroy the Calamarain before they destroy us,* he realized. A grim outcome to this mission, even assuming their foe could be extinguished somehow.

"They've heard you," Troi reported, sensing the Calamarain's reaction. "I think they're going to respond."

"Incoming transmission via tachyon emission," Data confirmed. He consulted his monitor and made a few quick adjustments to the translation program.

An eerie voice, devoid of gender or human inflections, echoed throughout the bridge. Riker decided he preferred the computer's ordinary tones, or even the harsh cadence of spoken Klingon.

"We/singular remain/endure the Calamarain," it intoned. "Moat is sacred/essential. No release/No escape. Chaos waits/threatens. Enterprise brings/succors chaos. Evaporation/sublimation is mandatory/preferable."

Riker scowled at the awkward and downright cryptic phrasing of the Calamarain's message. Unfortunately, Data didn't have nearly enough time to get all the bugs worked out of the new translation program. *It will have to do,* he resolved. Throughout human history, explorers and peacemakers had coped without any foolproof, high-tech translating devices. Could the crew of the *Enterprise* do any less?

When the Calamarain talked of "chaos," he guessed, they referred to Q and his kind. Frankly, he couldn't blame the Calamarain for mistrusting anyone associated with Q; that devilish troublemaker wasn't exactly the most sterling character witness. As for "evaporation/sublimation," he feared that term was simply the cloud creatures' way of describing the forthcoming destruction of the *Enterprise,* sublimation being the chemical process by which solid matter was reduced to a gaseous state. *Who knows?* he thought. *Maybe the Calamarain think they're doing us a favor by liberating our respective molecules from the constraints of solid existence.*

He didn't exactly see things their way. "Listen to me," he told the Calamarain, hoping that his own words weren't getting as badly garbled as theirs. He strove to keep his syntax as simple as possible. "The beings known as the Q Continuum are not our allies. We do not serve the Q."

In fact, he recalled, Q had also warned Captain Picard to stay away from the galactic barrier

"Chaos within/without," the Calamarain stated mysteriously. "Chaos then/now/to come. No/not be/not again. Excess risk/dread. No *Enterprise*/no be."

That doesn't sound good, Riker thought, *whatever it means.* He refused to give up, boiling his intended message down to its basics. "Please believe me. We will not harm you. Let us go." *Even our shaky translator can't mangle that,* he prayed.

The Calamarain responded not with words but with a roar of thunder that rocked the bridge. Riker felt his breath knocked out of him as the floor suddenly lurched to starboard, nearly toppling him from the captain's chair. Troi gasped nearby and fierce bolts of electrical fire arced across the viewscreen. At the conn, Ensign Clarze struggled to stabilize their flight path; sweat beaded on his smooth, hairless skull. Behind Riker, Lieutenant Leyoro held on to the tactical podium for dear life while the rest of the bridge staff fought to remain at their stations. Only Data looked unfazed by the abrupt jolt. "The Calamarain are not replying to your last transmission, Commander," he reported. The android inspected the raging tempest on the screen. "At least not verbally."

Troi released her grip on her chair's armrests as

the floor leveled. The din of the Calamarain's attack persisted, though, like a ringing in Riker's ears and a constant vibration through his bones. "I sense great impatience," she informed him. "They're through with talking, Will."

"I got that impression," he said. He looked around the bridge at the tense and wary faces of the men and women depending on his leadership. *Wherever you are, Captain,* he thought, *I hope you're faring better than us.*

Chapter Two

"Now where are we?" he asked. "And when?"

Captain Jean-Luc Picard, late of the *Starship Enterprise*, looked around as he found himself drifting in deep space. An astounding abundance of stars surrounded him on all sides, more than he had ever seen from a single location before. Just by twisting his neck from side to side, he could spot an astonishing variety of stellar phenomena: giant pillars of dust and gas rising up into the starry void, great globular clusters filled with millions of shining blue suns, supernovas spewing light and matter in their violent death throes, nebulas, quasars, pulsars, and more. Craning his head back, he saw above him what looked like the awesome spectacle of two enormous clouds of stars colliding; huge glowing spirals, streaked with shades of blue and scarlet and bedecked with countless specks of white-hot fire, merged into an amorphous mass of luminescence large enough, Picard guessed, to hold—or destroy—several million solar systems. Were any of those worlds inhabited? he wondered, hoping despite all appearances that some form of sentient life could survive the tremendous cosmic cataclysm transpiring overhead. Then Q drifted between Picard and the fusing stellar clusters, completely spoiling the view.

"Quite a show, isn't it?" Q remarked, floating on his back with his interlocked hands cradling the back of his head, his elbows extended toward the sky. Like Picard, he wore only a standard Starfleet uniform, his omniscience protecting them both from the vacuum. "You should have seen it the first time."

Impressive, yes, Picard agreed silently, but where exactly, in space *and* time were they now? As he floated in the void, he considered all that he saw around him. Judging from the sheer density of stars in sight, he theorized that he and Q were either very close to the galactic core of the Milky Way or else sometime very distant in the past, when the expanding universe was much smaller, and the interstellar distances much shorter, than they were in his own time. Or both, he realized.

"When is this?" he asked Q again. At the preceding stop on Q's tour, Picard had found himself millions of years in the past. He could only speculate what era Q had brought him to now, just as he could only ponder what devious reason Q had for abducting him in the first place. Besides Q's own perverse amusement, that is. "I demand an explanation."

"One would think you would have learned by now, *mon capitaine,*" Q replied, "that your demands and desires are quite irrelevant where I am concerned." He assumed a standing posture a few meters away from Picard. "For what it's worth, though, we are presently a mere one million years before your home sweet home in the twenty-fourth century." A polished bronze pocketwatch materialized in Q's palm and he squinted at its face. "Hmmm. We seem to be a few minutes early."

"Early for what?" Picard asked. At every previous stop, they had observed the activities of Q's younger self. Yet they appeared to be very much alone at the present, with only a surplus of stars to keep them company. *A million years ago,* he thought, both amazed and aghast. *Even if I knew where Earth was among those distant stars, the first human beings will not stand erect for another five hundred thousand years. Here and now, I am the only living* Homo sapiens *in the entire universe.* It was a terrifying thought.

"For them," Q answered as a sudden flash of white light attracted Picard's eyes. The light flared and died in an instant, leaving behind two humanoid figures striding across the empty void as though they were walking upon a level pathway. They approached him and Q at a brisk pace, coming within ten or fifteen meters of where Picard floated beside Q. Paradoxically, he thought he heard footsteps, despite the utter absurdity of any sound existing in the vacuum. *Then again,* he thought, *with Q, nothing is impossible.*

He recognized both figures from earlier points in Q's past. One of them was Q himself, albeit a million years younger than the self-centered and thoroughly irritating individual who had kidnapped him only hours before. This was a more youthful Q, he had learned, one at the very onset of his mischievous career Would that the Continuum had curbed him way back here, Picard thought, knowing better than most just how insufferable Q would become in the many millennia ahead. *I don't know what's scarier,* he mused, *a more juvenile Q or a one closer to the Q I know.*

The other figure made Picard even more uneasy. He called himself 0, as in nil, and he claimed to be an explorer from a far-off dimension unknown even to the Continuum. Picard, who considered himself a quick judge of character, found 0 quite a shady customer. *Back on the* Enterprise, he thought, *I wouldn't trust him within a light-year of my starship.* Picard was quick to remember that everything he now saw had been "translated" by Q into terms his human mind and senses could comprehend. That being the case, Picard had to wonder what more-than-human characteristics were represented by 0's weathered features and stout frame, and how much the older Q's memories may have colored his anthropomorphized portrait of the roguish stranger. From what preternatural first impression came the devilish gleam in the man's azure eyes, the cocksure set of his toothy grin, or the swagger in his stride? Picard could tell 0 was trouble at first glance; so why couldn't the Q of this era? Just who or what *was* 0? Falstaff to the young Q's Prince Hal, Picard speculated, falling back as ever on his beloved Shakespeare, or something a good deal more sinister? *If nothing else, I'm accumulating valuable insights into the early days of the Q Continuum.* He just hoped that he would someday be able to return to his own ship and era so that he could report all he had learned back to Starfleet, where the Q were justly regarded as one of the universe's most intriguing mysteries—and potential threats.

As before, neither 0 nor the younger Q were aware of Q and Picard's presence. Much like Scrooge and his ghostly visitors, Picard thought, when they spied on the likes of Bob Cratchit or Fezziwig.

0 sang boisterously as he trod with spaceways with Q:

"There was a young lad whose bold virility,
brought him some pains in a court of civility."

The attire of the new arrivals, Picard noted, had changed significantly since 0's first appearance in this universe. This came as no surprise; throughout

Picard's trek through time, the clothing of those he observed had evolved more or less along Earth's historical lines. An artistic conceit, according to Q, intended to convey a sense of antiquity, as well as the gradual passage of time, to the likes of Picard, who had to wonder whether the concept of clothing even applied to the Q in their true form. *How much of this is real,* he mused, *and how much simply stage dressing on the part of Q?*

He might never know.

"On posh settees with pinky out,
He found not much to chat about."

At present, 0 and the young Q affected the fashions of eighteenth century Europe, some one hundred thousand millennia before the real thing. Both figures wore stylish velvet suits, 0's a rich olive green, while Q preferred periwinkle blue. Their long coats were open in front to expose rosy damask vests from which ruffled shirt tops peeked. Black silk cravats were tied around their necks and each man wore a short brown wig, tied in the back, atop his head. Polished black shoes with gleaming metal buckles clicked impossibly against the emptiness of space, beneath white wool stockings that were held up by ribbons tied above the knee. They might have been two fine gentlemen out for a night on the town, Picard observed, except that, in this instance, that town was the known universe of a million years ago.

0's singing voice was as gravelly as ever, and more enthusiastic than melodious:

"But on darkened nights, 'hind tavern gates,
He discovered he had lots of mates!"

Wrapping up his raucous ditty, he laughed and slapped young Q on the back. "Boldness!" 0 declared. "That's the ticket. Follow your instincts and never mind what the fainthearted say." His raspy voice held a trace of an accent that Picard couldn't place; certainly it was nothing resembling the captain's native French. 0's crippled left leg dragged behind him as he hiked beside Q, expounding on a topic he had mentioned before. "Take the fine art of testing, say. Determining the ultimate limits and potential of lesser species under controlled conditions. That's a fine and fitting vocation for beings like us. Who better than we to invent curious and creative challenges for our brutish brethren?"

"It sounds fascinating," young Q admitted. "I've always been intrigued by primitive life-forms, especially those with a crude approximation of sentience, but it never occurred to me to intervene in their humble existences. I've simply observed them in their natural environments."

"That's fine for a start," 0 said, "but you can't really understand a species unless you've seen how they respond to completely unexpected circumstances—of the sort that only we can provide. It's an engrossing pastime for us, entertaining as well as educational, while providing a valuable service to the multiverse. Only by testing baser breeds can they be forced to transcend their wretched routines and advance to the next level of existence." 0 lifted his gaze heavenward as he extolled this lofty agenda. "Or not," he added with a shrug.

"But doesn't meddling with their petty lives interfere with their natural evolution?" Q asked. Picard's jaw nearly dropped at the sight of Q making the case for the Prime Directive. *Now I've seen everything,* he thought.

"Nature is overrated," 0 insisted. "We can do better." A gold-framed mirror appeared out of nowhere and 0 held it out in front of him so that it captured the reflection of both him and Q. "Take you and me, say. Do you think our far-seeing forebears would have ever evolved to this exalted state if they'd worried about what nature intended? Of course not! We've overcome our base, bestial origins, so it's only fitting that we help other breeds do the same—if they're able."

"And if they're not?" Q asked.

0 dispatched the mirror to oblivion, then shrugged. "Well, that's regrettable when it happens, but you can't groom a garden without doing a little pruning now and then. Extinction's part of the evolutionary agenda, natural or not. Some portion of those beneath us are going to flunk the survival test whether we help them along or not. We're just applying a little creativity to the process."

Picard recalled the older Q's periodic attempts to judge humanity and felt a chill run down his spine. Was this where Q acquired his fondness for draconian threats? If so, he thought, then 0 had a lot to answer for.

"That's true enough, I suppose," the young Q said, listening attentively and occasionally nodding in agreement. To Picard's dismay, 0's lessons appeared to be sinking in. "I take it you've done this before?"

"Here and there," 0 admitted with what Picard regarded as characteristic vagueness. "But you don't need to take my word for it, not when you can experience for yourself the rich and restorative rewards of such pursuits. And there's no time like this moment to begin," he enthused, giving Q a hearty slap on the back while simultaneously, Picard noted, changing the subject from his past to the present. "Now, where are these peculiar people you were telling me about?"

Young Q pointed at the colliding star clusters overhead. Lace cuffs protruded from the deep, turned-back sleeves of his velvet coat. "Look!" he urged 0, and Picard was surprised by the infectious good humor in the youth's tone, so different from the sour sarcasm of his older self. "Here they come."

Picard looked where indicated. At first he saw nothing but the same breathtaking panorama he had viewed before, the luminous swirls of stars and radiant gas coming together into one resplendent pageant of light and color, but as he gazed further a portion of the colossal spectacle seemed to detach itself from the whole, growing ever larger in comparison as it hurled across the void toward the assembled immortals, plus Picard. The strange phenomenon devoured the incalculable distance between them, coming closer and closer until he recognized the incandescent cloud of seething plasma.

"The Calamarain," Picard breathed in astonishment, never mind the lack of any visible atmosphere. And one million years in the past, no less! He never would have imagined that the Calamarain were so old. Were these the very same entities who had been approaching the *Enterprise* before, at the very moment that Q had snatched him away, or were these merely their remote ancestors? Either way, who could have guessed that their kind dated back to so distant an era?

Then again, he reflected, the late Professor Galen's archaeological studies had revealed, with a little help from the captain himself, that humanoid life existed in the Milky Way galaxy as far back as four billion years ago, and Picard had recently seen with his own eyes humanoid beings on Tagus III two billion years before his own time, so why should he be surprised that gaseous life-forms were at least one million years old? Picard shook his head numbly; the tremendous spans of time encompassed by his journey were almost too huge to conceive of, let alone keep track of. *It's too much,* he thought, trying to roll with the conceptual punches Q kept dishing out. *How can one mortal mind cope with time on this scale?*

The massive cloud that was the Calamarain, larger and wider across than even a Sovereign-class starship, passed within several kilometers of Picard, 0, and the two Qs. Iridescent patterns dazzled along the length and breadth of the cloud, producing a kaleidoscopic array of surging hues and shades. "So these are them?" 0 said, the wrinkles around his eyes deepening as he peered at the huge accumulation of vapors. "Well, they're sparkly enough, I'll give them that." His nostrils flared as he sniffed the vacuum. "They smell like a swamp, though." He limped nearer to the border of the cloud. "What say we start the testing with them, see how adaptable they are?"

"Er, I'm not sure that's a good idea," young Q answered, lagging behind. One of his high stockings came loose and he tugged haplessly at its neck. Next to Picard, his older self sighed and shook his head sadly. "The Coulalakritous are fairly advanced in their own right, only a few levels below the Continuum, and they aren't exactly the most sociable of creatures."

"Coulalakritous?" Picard whispered to his own Q, lowering his voice out of habit even though neither 0 nor the young Q could hear him.

"The name changed later," he said, shrugging his

shoulders. "Be reasonable, Jean-Luc. It's been umpteen thousand years, after all. How often do you think of your precious France as Gaul?"

Picard decided not to argue the point, choosing instead to concentrate on the scenario unfolding before him. So this was indeed where Q first acquired his insidious inclination for "testing" humanity and other species. *Many thanks, 0,* he thought bitterly; if the mysterious entity did nothing else, this alone was enough to condemn him in Picard's eyes.

"Wait," young Q called out, hurrying to catch up with his companion as 0 continued to advance toward the sentient plasma cloud. "I told you, they don't approve of visitors."

"And you're going to let that stop you?" 0 challenged. He chuckled and stirred the outside of the cloud with a meaty finger. Thin blue tracings of bioelectrical energy ran up his arm, but he only cackled louder. "All the more reason to shake up their insular existence and see how they react. You'll never learn anything if you worry about what the subject of your experiment wants. Let the tested dictate the terms of the test and you defeat the whole point of the exercise."

"I don't know," young Q said, hesitating. Picard thought he saw restraint and good sense warring with temptation and unchecked curiosity on the callow godling's face. *I know which side I'm betting on,* he thought, calling upon over ten years of personal experience with the older Q.

"Come on, friend," 0 egged him on. "Surely we didn't come all this way just to gawk at these cumulus critters from out here. Where's your sense of adventure, not to mention scientific inquiry?"

Restraint and good sense went down in flames as the young Q's pride asserted itself. "Right here!" he crowed, thumbing his chest. "Who are these puffed-up piles of hot air to decide where a Q should come and go? To blazes with their privacy!"

"There's the Q I know!" 0 said proudly, and Picard, looking on silently, had to agree. 0 jabbed his protégé in the ribs with his elbow. "For a second there I thought you might be one of those stuffed shirts from the Continuum." His face assumed a mock-serious expression that endured for only an instant before collapsing into a mischievous grin. "Between you and me, friend, you're the only one of your lot with any fire or fission at all, not to mention a sense of humor."

"Don't I know it!" young Q said indignantly. He backed up to take a running leap into the glowing cloudmass. "Last one into the Coulalakritous is a—"

0 grabbed Q's collar as he ran by, only moments before the impetuous super-being dived headlong into the sentient plasma. "Not so fast," he counseled Q, confusing his duly appointed guardian. "No reason to go barging in there, especially if this phosphorescent fog is as inhospitable as you give me to believe." A crafty smile creased his face. "I say we infiltrate them first. The testing is always

more accurate if the tester's hand remains concealed, especially at the beginning."

Showing his true colors, Picard thought. Alas, the starstruck young Q failed to make the connection between 0's plan to deceive the Coulalakritous and the way 0 had already inveigled his way into Q's trust—and, through him, the Continuum.

"Just follow my lead, young Q, and keep your wits about you." Like a genie returning to his bottle, 0 dissolved into a pocket of phosphorescent mist indistinguishable from that which composed the Coulalakritous. He/it hovered for a second outside the immense cloud, then flowed tailfirst into the billowing vapors as though sucked in by some powerful pumping mechanism. The young Q gulped nervously, looking back over his shoulder as if contemplating a hasty retreat, but soon underwent the same transformation and followed his would-be mentor into the mass of plasma. Picard made an attempt to keep track of the two new streams of gas, but it was like trying to discern an individual splash of liquid within a restless ocean. From where Picard was floating, 0 and young Q were completely lost within the Coulalakritous. Their metamorphosis surprised him at first, but the logic behind it was readily apparent. *If Q assumes human form when he tests humanity, I suppose it only follows that he and 0 would disguise themselves as gases before testing the Coulalakritous.*

"Hard to imagine I was ever so suggestible," the

older Q commented, but Picard felt more apprehensive than nostalgic. His heart sank as he guessed what was coming next.

"We're going after them, aren't we?" he asked, resigned to yet another bizarre and disorienting experience. *At least I might learn something that could help the* Enterprise *in my own time,* he consoled himself, assuming his ship had indeed encountered the Calamarain in his absence. It dawned on him that he had no idea how much time might have passed upon the *Enterprise* while he was away. Had the Calamarain threatened the ship once more? What was happening to Riker and the others?

"You know me so well, Jean-Luc," Q said. He snapped his fingers and a sudden hot flush rushed over Picard as, before his eyes, the very atoms of his body sped up and drifted farther apart, their molecular bonds dissolving at Q's direction. He held his hand up before his face just in time to see the hand become insubstantial and semitransparent, like a ghost in some holodeck fantasy. His fingers fluttered like smoke rising from a five-year-old's birthday cake, merging and coalescing into a single continuous stream of radiant mist. His arm quickly went the way of his digits and, before he knew it, Picard saw within his field of vision only the outer limits of the man-sized accumulation of gas he had become.

How can I see without eyes? he marveled. *How*

can I think without a brain? But the Calamarain, or the Coualalakritous, or whatever they were called at this place and time, proved that consciousness could exist in this form, so he could, too, it seemed. The galaxy looked the same as it had before, the overflowing cornucopia of stars around him shining just as brightly. He felt a strange energy suffusing his being, though, like the tingle of static electricity before it was discharged. Strange new senses, feeling like a cross between hearing and touch, detected waves of power radiating from the Coualalakritous. The charge of the larger cloud tugged on him like gravity, drawing him toward the seething sea of vapor. Picard surrendered to the pull, uncertain how he could have fled even if he had wanted to. Despite his resignation, a sudden sense of misgiving increased as the great cloud filled the horizon. He felt a surge of panic welling from somewhere deep inside him, and realized that it stemmed from his memories of being immersed in the group-mind of the Borg Collective. If he had still possessed a physical body, he would have trembled at the prospect of losing his individuality once again.

Another shimmering cloudlet drifted a few meters away, on a parallel course toward the Coualalakritous. Lacking a mouth or any other features, it nonetheless addressed him in Q's voice. "Be of stout heart, Picard. You're going where no vaporized human has ever gone before."

Then the stars were gone and all Picard could see or hear or feel was the overwhelming presence of the cosmic cloud all around him. It was a maelstrom of surging currents and eddies, carrying him along in their wake. A million voices hummed around him, yet, to his vast relief, he discovered he could still isolate his own thoughts from the din. Snatches of conversation, too many to count, beat upon his new inhuman senses, almost deafening him:

. . . *the Principal Intent of Gravitational Fixities are to perpetuate Substance along Graduated Hierarchies . . . until fuller Thou art, tarry and ask Myself again . . . to the Inverse, the Singular Attributes of Transuranic Essentials plainly denote . . . Solitary Pygmy Suns forever desired before Paired Twins . . . no, Thou mistakes My Supposition grossly . . . ever should the Whole of Thoughtful Souls arrive at Concord and Harmony . . . much does Myself long to behold Such . . . never in Tenfold Demi-Spans shall That come to pass . . . should Thou refuse to merge Thy Vitality with Thy Fellows, Thou cannot rightly anticipate that They shall merge Thine with Thou . . . Our Hours were Exemplary in the Time Before . . . was a Unique Instance, not a Tendency of Import or Duration . . . I dreamed I was a Fluid . . . wherefore do We journey? . . . entreat Succor for Myself, My Ions lose Their Galvanism . . . Thou ever avers Such! . . . the Pursuit of Grace takes precedence over Mere*

Beauty . . . do Thou fancy that Quasars have
Spirits? . . . I dispute That resolutely . . . no, pray
regard the Evidence. . . .

Mon Dieu, Picard thought, spellbound by the
unending torrent of communication, which struck
him as being somewhere halfway between a Vulcan
mind-meld and late-night debates at Starfleet
Academy. As far as he could tell, the Coulalakritous did not possess a single unified consciousness like the Borg, but rather were engaged in
incessant dialogue with each other. Could it be, he
speculated, that this sentient cloudmass represented some form of absolute democracy? Or perhaps they had a more academic orientation, like an
incorporeal university or seminar. He wondered
how this incredible forum compared with the
Great Link of the Changelings, as described in
Odo's intelligence reports from Deep Space Nine.
The so-called Founders were liquid while the Coulalakritous were gaseous, but how different did that
make the two species? From the point of view of a
former solid, he mused, both seem equally amorphous . . . and astounding. He could only hope
that someday he would have the opportunity to
compare the experiences with Odo himself. No
doubt Worf or Miles O'Brien would be happy to
introduce them.

"Annoying, aren't they?" Q's voice piped up
from somewhere nearby. "They never shut up and
they never tire of debating each other. Small wonder they don't want to communicate with any other

intelligences; they're too busy arguing with themselves."

Picard looked for Q, but all he saw was the ceaseless motion of the Coulalakritous. It seemed a minor miracle that he could hear Q at all over the cacophonous buzz of the cloud creatures' conversation. *These aren't really sound waves at all,* he considered, recalling a Starfleet theory that the Calamarain communicated by means of tachyon emissions. *Am I actually "hearing" tachyons now?*

The ambient heat within the cloud was intense, but his new form did not find it uncomfortable. Of course, he realized. The Coulalakritous would have to generate their own internal heat, and in massive quantities, to avoid freezing solid in the cold of space. Some sort of metabolic chemical reaction, he wondered, or controlled nuclear fusion? Either way, he suspected that his ordinary human body would be incinerated instantly by the volcanic temperature within the cloud. Instead, the ionized gases merely felt like a sauna or hot spring. Remarkable, Picard thought, savoring the experience despite other, more pressing concerns. The more he listened, the more he thought he could isolate individual voices by their tone or timbre. There were diverse personalities alive within the collective boundaries of the plasma cloud: long-winded bores, excited explorers, passionate visionaries, skeptics, cranks, poets, philosophers, fussbudgets, free thinkers, reactionaries, radicals, and scientists. He could hear them all, and the only thing they all seemed to have in common was that they savored debate and discussion. *There's so much we could learn from these beings,* Picard thought.

Q sounded substantially less awestruck. "If I live to be another eternity, I'll never understand why I found this nattering miasma so interesting in the first place." Picard could hear the impatience in his tone. "If you're quite through with your adolescent sense of wonder, perhaps you'd care to pay attention to the carefree antics of my younger self and his dubious acquaintance. That *is* why we're here, you know."

"Where are they?" Picard asked, genuinely at a loss.

"Can't you hear them?" Q responded. "Why, they're right over there."

Not only could Picard not distinguish 0 and the other Q from the rest of the maelstrom, he couldn't even see Q. No doubt the Coulalakritous could tell each other apart visually, he thought, but he could barely make sense of what he was hearing, let alone seeing. Even though he was beginning to distinguish one voice from another, he could hardly pinpoint two specific individuals in this gaseous Tower of Babel. The sights and sensations remained far too alien. "Over there? Pay attention?" he said, incredulous. "I don't even know what I am anymore."

"Complain, complain. Is that all you can do, Jean-Luc?" Q said. "I knew I should have brought along Data instead. At least he can listen to more than one sound at once and still comprehend what he's hearing." He sounded sorely ill-used. "Very well, I suppose I have to do *everything* around here."

All at once, the overpowering rustle of impassioned discussion surrounding him receded further into the background, to the extent that he could now isolate the distinctive voices of both 0 and the younger Q. The two counterfeit Coulalakritous became visible as well, acquiring a silvery metallic glow that set them apart from the other sentient gases swirling through the vast gaseous community. Shapeless and inhuman, they reminded Picard of globules of liquid mercury. He assumed that the silver tinting was for his benefit alone; presumably both the Coulalakritous and the trespassing immortals were unaware of the change. The argent glow had to be out of phase, too, lest he and the older Q's presence be exposed. To Picard's slight annoyance, he observed that his obnoxious traveling companion had not bothered to make himself visible as well. *It's just like Q,* he fumed, *to put others at a disadvantage, especially me.*

"Happy now?" the indistinguishable Q asked. He might have been anywhere around Picard. "Do try to concentrate, Jean-Luc. I don't want to have to relive this a third time just for your sake."

Conveniently, the silver puffs of vapor were not far away, although Picard found it hard to estimate precise distances within such an atypical environment. They were certainly within listening range.

He felt slightly uncomfortable eavesdropping this way, even on a Q, but he had to concede that it was preferable to having to deal with 0 and the other Q directly. Every Starfleet captain knew a little espionage was necessary now and then.

"Is this all they do?" 0 inquired out loud. His cloud, Picard noted, was larger than the younger Q's, and streaked with dark metallic shadings that were almost black in places. "Why, they're nothing but talk! Rancid and rubbish, all of them." He clearly did not approve.

"Well, they're said to have traveled extensively throughout the galaxy," his companion offered. At the moment, the youthful Q resembled a glistening dust devil, whirling madly with speed and energy to burn. "And they never forget anything, or so I'm told."

"Tell me about it," the older Q said dryly, possibly recalling the Calamarain's undying vendetta against him.

"Can they travel faster than a ray of sunlight?" 0 asked, and Picard could readily imagine the calculating expression on the old rogue's face. If 0 still had a humanoid face, that is.

"Why, sure! How else would they get around?" Q said cheerily, then remembered 0's inability to travel at warp speed except through the Continuum. "Er, nothing personal, I mean. I forgot about your . . . well, there's more to godhood than zipping from here to there in a hurry." The spinning cloud turned pink with embarrassment at his faux pas. "Why rush when you have all of eternity, right?"

This really was a long time ago, Picard realized. It was hard to imagine the Q of the twenty-fourth century being embarrassed by anything, let alone a tactless remark. *More's the pity,* he thought.

"Calm down, friend. No offense taken," 0 insisted. "This old wanderer's well aware of his present limitations. It's hardly your fault, Q." An edge of bitterness colored his words and Picard recalled the crippled leg 0 possessed in his human guise. "Blame instead those meddling miscreants who banished me here in the first place. Contemptible curs!"

"But I thought you came here of your own choosing," the Q-cloud said, taken aback by the sudden malevolence in 0's tone, the spin of its miniature eddies slowing anxiously.

"So I did!" 0 asserted, regaining his usual robust air. "Who says otherwise?"

"But, I mean, you . . ." Q stammered. Picard had to admit to himself that he found this Q's discomfort rather satisfying; it was good to see Q off balance for once, even if Picard had been forced to travel countless centuries in the past to witness the occasion.

"Yesterday's news," 0 insisted. "Moldy memories better off forgotten." The silver mist that was 0 cruised along the perimeter of the plasma cloud. Picard found he could follow him by focusing his attention in that direction. "Let's get on with the business of testing this talkative tempest. Here's an idea: Suppose we try to herd this cloud in one direction or another. Put some wind in our sails, so to speak."

"Er, what exactly would that prove?" Q asked.

"Why, nothing less than whether the Coulalakritous are capable—and worthy—of controlling their own destiny. If the likes of you and I have the power to change their course at will, then plainly they're not as highly evolved as they should be." He emitted the tachyon equivalent of a low chuckle. "And, as an added bonus, I acquire my own personal porters. What do you say, Q? Do you think we can do it?"

Mon Dieu, Picard thought, shocked by the cold-blooded ruthlessness of 0's suggestion. *He's thinking of enslaving the Coulalakritous, to harness them as means of faster-than-light transportation for himself!* It was a blatant violation of the Prime Directive, not to mention basic morality. The voices around him belonged to a sentient people, not beasts of burden. Did the young Q comprehend the full horror of what his companion was advocating? Picard wondered. Was this the telltale moment that would lift the scales from his (metaphorical) eyes?

Apparently not. "I don't know," young Q said. "I've never really considered the matter before."

"Of course not," 0 said readily. "Why should you, a healthy young Q like yourself?" The silver mist, with its darker undertones, oozed sinuously around the glowing pocket of gas that now embodied the young Q. "For us that have a wee bit of trouble getting around, though, this notion merits a closer look. After all, much as I enjoy your company, you don't want to have to chauffeur me around the cosmos indefinitely, do you?"

"That's what I promised the Continuum," Q said, sounding as if the full implications of that commitment were just now sinking in.

"So you did," 0 assented, "and for sure you meant it at the time." The volume of the dark silver gas began to increase dramatically, spreading out in all directions around the outer surface of the entire cloud. "Still, it can't hurt to explore other options now. You wanted to test another species, right? Trust me, this is as good a way as any."

"Wait. What are you doing?" The Q-mist started to churn anxiously within the confines of the elder entity's substance but found itself hemmed in, unable to move. "Stop it!"

"Just blasting two planets with one asteroid, that's all," 0 stated as his dark silver stain permeated the nebulous borders of the Coulalakritous, enclosing the cloud within his own gaseous grip. "Nothing to be alarmed about, at least not for you and me. The cloud, on the other hand . . . well, they might have cause for concern."

This is monstrous, Picard thought, sickened by 0's shameless attempt to place an entire community of intelligent beings under his control. If he understood the situation correctly, 0 meant to turn the Coulalakritous into the interstellar equivalent of galley slaves, yoked into transporting 0 throughout the galaxy at warp speed. He had to remind himself that, whatever happened next, everything he was witnessing now had already taken place from the perspective of his own era, was incredibly ancient history in fact, predating the very birth of humanity, none of which made it any easier to watch. "Why didn't you do something?" he challenged the older Q, wherever he was.

"It was too new," Q apologized from somewhere behind Picard. *"I* was too new. 0 sounded like he knew what he was doing. How was I supposed to know whether it was a reasonable experiment or not?"

"How could you not have?" Picard answered angrily. Humanity had already learned that such exploitation of another intelligent species was unconscionable, and human history was only a nanosecond in the lifetime of Q if his most grandiose claims were to believed. "What's so hard to understand about slavery?"

"Ever ridden a horse, Picard?" Q retorted. "Ever bred bees for honey? Believe me, you're a lot closer to a horse or a bug than I was to the Coualalakritous, even back then. Don't be so quick to judge me."

"These are not horses!" the captain said. Indignation deepened his voice. "And they are most certainly not insects. I've heard them, felt them, experienced at least a fragment of their existence—and so have you."

"I've listened to you, too, Picard," Q said, materializing before Picard in his usual guise. He pinched the fabric of his uniform. "Contrary to my appearance, that doesn't make me human, or even a humanitarian."

Picard would have shaken his head in disgust had he still possessed humanoid form. *I don't know why I should be so surprised,* he thought. *Q has never shown any consideration for "lesser" species before, and it seems he was always that way.*

By now the taint of 0 had spread all over the exterior of the cloud community. It thickened and solidified, enclosing the Coulalakritous within a thin, silvery membrane that began to squeeze inward, forcing the assembled gases (including Picard) to flow only in the direction 0 had chosen. But his efforts to take the reins of the cloud did not go unnoticed.

The perpetual buzz of a million voices fell silent for an instant, thousands upon thousands of discussions interrupted simultaneously, before the dialogue started up again with a new and more urgent tone:

what is This? . . . What Now transpires? . . . Make It cease! . . . Fearful am I . . . I cannot touch the Outside! . . . Nor I . . . Nor I . . . hurts Myself . . . crushing . . . so Cold . . . losing Vitality . . . cannot move . . . cease . . . cease NOW! . . .

It was hideous. Within seconds, 0 had reduced an ageless, living symposium to panic. Picard heard the shock and dismay in the cries of the entire assemblage. He longed for the *Enterprise,* whose powerful phasers might be able to surgically peel 0 away from the Coulalakritous, but his ship was many millennia away. *If only I could do something to help these people!*

0 laughed boisterously, drowning out Picard's frustrated craving to stop him. The membrane squeezed harder and Picard felt the compressed gases press in on him from all sides but one, propelling him forward against his will. "Wait," he protested, not understanding why he should be feeling any pressure at all. "I thought we were out of phase with this moment in time."

"Poetic license," Q explained, his humanoid shape unaffected by the pressure. "I want you to get the full experience."

In other words, Picard realized, Q was generating the sensation himself, to simulate conditions within the besieged cloud of plasma. Picard was less than grateful. *I could have easily done without this much verisimilitude.*

The Coulalakritous fought back. Overcoming their initial consternation, the voices began to come together with a single purpose:

. . . cease . . . halt the Adversary . . . Our Volition is Our Own . . . Our Will is United . . . cease crushing Us . . . hurts . . . disregard the Torment . . . shall not yield . . . persevere, do not cease stirring, All of We . . . Halt the Cold . . . do not be Fearful . . . Ours is the Heat of Many is . . . must be Free . . . persevere . . . Together We can break free . . . Together We . . . together . . . Flashes of

lightning sparked along the inner skin of the membrane 0 had become. . . . *Together . . . Together . . . Together . . .*

"Are you indeed?" 0 mocked them, his voice emerging from the membrane so that he seemed to be speaking from all directions at once. "All unanimity aside, I believe I have the upper hand at the moment," he said, demonstrating his point by constricting the enclosed gases further. Picard lost sight of the Q-mist as, poetic license or not, he felt his substance stretched and prodded by the pressure being exerted on the cloud community. Because his senses were distorted by his unlikely new form, it felt like a scream and sounded like heavy gravity. Claustrophobia gripped him now that he could no longer flow freely through the great cloud, and he marveled at how quickly he had grown accustomed to his gaseous state. At least he was used to being contained within a skin of flesh; he could only imagine how unbearable this captivity must be to the Coulalakritous. *If only I could do something,* he thought, *but I'm not even really here . . . I think.*

The cloud-beings did not submit readily to 0's will. The atmosphere surrounding Picard warmed dramatically, transforming into a cauldron of superheated gases, as they expanded outward against the pressure of the membrane. The swirling maelstrom of sentient vapors increased in fury, gaining strength and intensity by the moment. Picard had a sudden mental image of being in the middle of—

no, being *part of*—an old-fashioned steam engine of colossal proportions. *Perhaps,* he thought hopefully, *0 has underestimated the Coulalakritous.* After all, they surely hadn't endured into the twenty-fourth century, eventually evolving into the Calamarain, by being defenseless. He cheered on their efforts, wishing he could add his own determination, out of phase as he was, to the struggle.

. . . Together . . . break   free . . . Together . . . break   free . . . Together . . . break   free . . . Together . . . break free . . . Together . . .

Slowly, the tide appeared to turn. The cloud swelled against the membrane, spreading it ever thinner around an expanding volume of ionized and agitated gas. "Beasts! Brutes! Upstarts!" 0 cursed them, but his voice faded in volume as his width approached infinitesimal. Within the cloud, fierce currents tossed Picard around like a cork upon the waves. "Blast you," 0 raged, barely audible now. "Give up, why don't you? Surrender!"

Then, like an overinflated balloon, the membrane that was 0 came apart and the victorious Coulalakritous rushed through the gap to freedom. "Time to switch seats for a better view," the older Q commented, and Picard abruptly found himself outside the cloud, looking on from a distance. The gigantic fog, even larger and more diffuse than before, loomed ahead of him, so attenuated that Picard could glimpse stars and nebulae through it. The Coulalakritous wasted no time contracting back to their original proportions, growing opaque once more. A second later, a stream of silver mist was forcibly ejected from the vaporous community. "Not my most dignified exit," Q commented, watching his younger self spew forth from the interior of the Coulalakritous, "but I like to think I've improved since. You must concede that I've always managed to depart the *Enterprise* with more than a modicum of style."

"I have always savored your exits," Picard couldn't resist replying, "more than any other aspect of your visits." Now that they had left the plasma cloud behind, they had both resumed human form. Picard was relieved to look down and see his body once more. Given a choice, he discovered he preferred floating adrift in space to squeezing in among the Coulalakritous.

"Ho, ho, Jean-Luc," Q said darkly, hanging upside down in relation to Picard. "Very droll. It would be too much to expect, I suppose, any sign of gratitude for showing you glimpses of a higher reality."

"Not when your motive has always seemed to be more about your own self-aggrandizement than my enlightenment," Picard answered.

"My self can't possibly be more aggrandized," Q stated, "as I thought you would have understood by now." He looked away from Picard at what remained of 0, hovering about a dozen meters away. "Watch closely, *mon capitaine*. Here's where things get *really* interesting."

Reduced to a severed string of silver-black film, 0

rapidly reconstituted himself, assuming the same human form he had affected before. His craggy face was flushed with anger and his once-fine clothes were charred and seared around their edges. Smoke rose symbolically from the anomalous male figure suspended in the vacuum of space; Picard could not tell whether the fumes emanated from 0's garments or his person. Beyond a doubt, 0 looked irritated enough to spontaneously combust at any moment.

His companion and guardian, the young Q, metamorphosized from mist to humanoid appearance, then strolled across the void toward 0. His attire was less battle-scarred than the other's, Picard noted, perhaps because Q had not attempted to subdue the Coulalakritous. Nervously eyeing his cohort's affronted demeanor, he seemed inclined to laugh the whole business off as an inconsequential lark. "Well, it appears we've worn out our welcome, and then some," he remarked flippantly. "Their loss, then. It's hardly the first time a lesser species has failed to appreciate a superior life form."

"Nor would it be the last," his older self added, with a pointed look at Picard.

"On that you and I can agree," Picard shot back, feeling singularly unappreciative at the moment.

The young Q's attempt at levity failed to assuage 0's ire. "They can't do this!" he snarled, his previously jovial mask slipping away to expose a visage of unmistakable indignation. "I won't be banished again, not by their sort." His pale blue eyes glittered like icy gems, reflecting the luminous shimmer of the Coulalakritous. "Never again," he swore. "Never, I say!"

Taken aback by 0's pique, young Q squirmed uncomfortably, uncertain how to deal with his friend's temper. "But didn't they pass your test?" he asked. "You tried to harness them. They wouldn't let you. I thought that was the whole point of the endeavor."

"They cheated!" 0 barked. "Just like the others. And if there's one thing that I never abide, it's a cheater. Remember that, Q, if you remember nothing else. Never allow cheaters to make a travesty of your tests."

"Cheated how?" Q asked, looking genuinely puzzled. "Did I miss something? As I much as I loathe admitting my ignorance, I am rather new at this, so I suppose it's possible I missed a subtlety or two. Perhaps you can explain what precisely they did wrong?"

If 0 was listening at all to Q's prattle, he gave no sign of it. He glared at the incandescent majesty of the Coulalakritous with undisguised hostility. He took a deep breath, inhaling some manner of sustenance from the ether, and appeared to be drawing on a hidden reserve of strength. The smoky gray fumes rising from his scorched garments entwined about each other and, from Picard's vantage point nearby, 0's human facade appeared to flicker slightly, giving Picard brief, almost subliminal glimpses of another, more inhuman form. He received an impression of something dark and coiled, surrounded by a blurry aura of excess limbs or tendrils. Or was that only an illusion created by the twisting spirals of smoke? The more he watched, the more Picard became convinced that what he saw was no mere trick of smoke and starlight, but a genuine glimpse of another aspect of the enigmatic stranger. Picard's Starfleet training, along with years of experience in dealing with diverse life-forms, had taught him not to judge other beings by their appearance; nonetheless, he could not repress a shudder at this transitory look behind 0's customary persona. Indeed, he reflected, it was the very indistinctness of the images he perceived that made them far more eerie and unsettling than a clear and distinct depiction of the alien would have been. Picard found his imagination all too eager to fill in the blanks in this fractional, impressionistic portrait of 0's true nature. *I knew there was more to him than met the eye,* he thought. *Why couldn't Q see that?*

Power radiated from 0 like a gust of chilling wind. Picard felt the passage of the energy upon his face, stinging his cheeks, yet the power was not directed at him but at the imposing presence of the Coulalakritous. What could 0 do to such magnificent entities? Picard wondered. Had not the Coulalakritous already demonstrated their ability to defend themselves?

Yet, to his horror, he beheld the huge plasma

cloud begin to shrink beneath 0's assault, its expansive volume diminishing by the second. The billowing gases slowed and thickened, the swirling eddies coming to a halt. Picard was only mildly surprised to discover that he could still hear the varied voices of the Coulalakritous crying out in distress, their words slurred and winding down like a malfunctioning recording:

no . . . nooo . . . noooo . . . not . . . anewwww . . . ceassse . . . sooooo . . . cooooold . . . stopppppp . . . traaaaaap . . . noooooo . . . essssscaaaaaape . . . ceasssssse . . . at . . . onccccccce . . . ceassssse . . . freeeeeezzzing . . . helppppppp . . .

"Yes, stop!" young Q seconded anxiously. "You don't need to do this, 0. Whatever they did, they're not worth our attention, let alone your peace of mind." His gaze darted back and forth between 0 and his imploding target. "Er, you can stop anytime now, anytime at all. . . ."

The enraged immortal paid no heed to either Q or the Coulalakritous. His hate-filled eyes protruded from their sockets while phantom tentacles wavered in and out of reality around him. A trickle of saliva dripped from the corner of his mouth as he ground his broad white teeth together. All his effort and concentration were aimed without exception at the intangible community that had possessed the audacity to elude his control. 0 raised his arms, an action echoed by a blur of black extensions, and coruscating scarlet energy flashed about his extended fingertips.

The cloud of plasma had already contracted to at least one-third its original size. It no longer looked truly gaseous in nature, but more like a mass of steaming, semiliquid slush. Then the slush congealed further, sucking in the last retreating wisps of vapor and turning a dull, ugly brown in hue. Picard had a horrifying mental image of an oppressed prisoner being crammed into a box far too small for him, as he watched, helpless to intervene, while 0 forced the entire awesome accumulation of gas-beings ever closer to a solid state.

. . . *Weeeeeee willlllllll nottttttttt forrrrrgettttttttt . . .* the Coualakritous vowed, their separate voices finally merging into one before falling silent entirely. Where only moments before had existed an incandescent cloud of blazing plasma, there now remained only a dense, frozen snowball, indistinguishable from any of a billion comets traversing the dark between the stars. *If they registered on the* Enterprise*'s sensors in this state,* Picard guessed, *we wouldn't give them a moment's thought.* Were the Coualakritous still conscious and aware of their utter paralysis? Part of Picard prayed that they were not.

Yet 0 was not satisfied. His beefy hands curled into grasping claws, he brought them closer together above his head, as if literally squeezing the onetime cloud between his palms instead of merely empty space. His phantasmal other self, superimposed upon his humanoid shell, shadowed his every move. Less than a kilometer away from 0, the inert chunk of ice that was the Coulalakritous kept on being compressed by invisible forces, its crystalline surface cracking and collapsing inward beneath the crushing power exerted by the vengeful immortal. How far did 0 intend to take this? Picard wondered, aghast. Until the very atoms that composed the Coulalakritous fused together, igniting a miniature supernova? Or was 0 able and willing to compress his victims' mass to so great a density that the Coulalakritous would be reduced to a microscopic black hole, a pinprick in reality from which they could never escape? Was such a horrendous feat even possible?

Young Q appeared to fear something along those lines. "I think that's enough, 0," he announced with unexpected firmness. With a burst of pure energy, he placed himself between 0 and his prey, grunting involuntarily as he felt the force of 0's unchecked ire. The flesh upon his face rippled and grew distorted, like that of an old-time astronaut enduring tremendous G-forces, and his bones crunched together noisily as he shrunk into a slightly squatter, more compact Q, losing at least a centimeter of height. He held his ground, though, and 0's attack rebounded upon its source, staggering the older entity and sending him stumbling backward through empty space. *Q to the rescue?* Picard marveled, more than a little startled by this atypical display of altruism. *I mean, of all people . . . Q?*

"What?" 0 was as taken aback by Q's actions as

Picard. "Are you out of your all-knowing mind?" he bellowed, visibly dismayed by the young Q's defiance. His ruddy face grew even more crimson. A vein along his left temple throbbed rhythmically like a pulsar. "Get out of my way, or I swear I'll . . . I'll . . ."

Q flinched in anticipation of the other's wrath, but no explosion, verbal or literal, followed. Perhaps caught off guard by his own angry words, 0 faltered, falling mute even as the flailing, insubstantial tendrils that enshrouded him withdrew into some private hiding place deep within his person. He turned his back on Q and the two invisible onlookers while he struggled to regain his composure. "0?" the young Q inquired anxiously.

When the stranger, his clothes still smoldering from his first battle with the Coulalakritous, faced them again, no trace of animosity could be found in his expression. He looked contrite and abashed, not to mention exhausted by his exertions. Perspiration plastered his damp curls to his skull. "Forgive me, friend, for losing my temper that way. I shouldn't have raised my voice to you, no matter how vexed that malodorous miasma made me."

"Never mind me," Q responded, stretching his body until he regained his usual dimensions. He looked back over his shoulder at the solidified chunk of Coulalakritous tumbling through the void, its momentum carrying the frigid comet slowly toward them. "What in the name of the Continuum have you done to them?"

0 paused to catch his breath before replying. Freezing the gas-beings had obvious taken a lot out of him. All the blood had drained from his face, leaving him drawn and pale. Lungs heaving, he bent forward, hands on his knees, and stared at his shoes until his color returned. "That?" he inquired, short of breath. "A mere bit of thermodynamic sleight-of-hand, and nothing those cantankerous clouds didn't have coming to them." He limped across the vacuum until he hovered only a few meters away from his fretful protégé. "You have to understand, Q, that in any tests there must be penalties for failure, and for deliberate cheating, or else there's no inducement to excel. It looks harsh, I know, but it's the only way. Lesser lights are not going to submit to our tests out of the goodness of their hearts. They seldom comprehend, you see, the honor and the opportunity being bestowed upon them. You need to *motivate* them, and sometimes that means having the gumption to apply a sharp poke when necessary."

"But the Coulalakritous?" Q asked, sounding baffled. "What exactly did they—"

"Things didn't go off quite as I planned there," 0 interrupted, striking a conciliatory tone. "To be honest, I underestimated how out of practice I am, and how inexperienced you are." He saw Q bristle at the remark and held up his hand to fend off the younger being's objections. "No criticism intended, friend, merely a statement of fact. I'm the one at fault for dropping us both into the deep end before we were ready. Perhaps we should round up some able assistance before trying again." He scratched his chin thoughtfully as the approaching ball of ice, roughly the size of a Starfleet shuttle-craft, barreled helplessly toward the location where he and Q just happened to be standing. "Yes, extra hands, that's the ticket. And I know just the right reinforcements to enlist in our cause. . . ."

"Reinforcements?" Q asked, seconds before the frozen Coulalakritous would have collided with the two humanoid figures. Neither seemed particularly concerned about the oncoming comet. "Who do you mean?"

"Wait and see," 0 promised. With a casual wave of his hand, he deflected the course of the tumbling mass of petrified plasma and sent it hurling off at a forty-five-degree angle from him and his compan-ion. "Follow me, Q. You won't be disappointed." He vacated the scene in a flash, taking the young Q with him. Left behind, Picard watched as the victimized Coulalakritous receded into the dis-tance. The closest star, the nearest possible source of warmth, was countless light-years away.

"It took them a couple millennia to thaw out again," Q whispered in his ear. He glanced down at the bronze pocketwatch in his hand. "Not that they learned anything from the experience. They're still just as ill-mannered as before."

Picard was appalled. Small wonder the Cala-marain had been eager to exact their revenge on Q back in the twenty-fourth century. "That's all you have to say about it?" Picard demanded, offended by Q's cavalier tone. "An entire species frozen into suspended animation for heaven knows how long, and you have the audacity to complain about their manners? Didn't this atrocity teach you anything? How could you not have realized how dangerous this 0 creature was?"

"Oh, don't overdramatize, Jean-Luc," Q replied, a tad more defensively than usual. "Perhaps I was a trifle blind, in an omniscient sort of way, but ultimately it was a mere prank, nothing more. A trifle mean-spirited, I concede, but there was no real harm done, not permanently. In the grand cosmic scheme of things, our ionized friends were merely inconvenienced, not actually injured in any way that need concern us here." He shrugged his shoulders. "Can I help it if the Calamarain didn't see the funny side of it?"

"If what I witnessed just now was nothing more than a prank," Picard declared indignantly, "then I shudder to think what you would consider genuine maliciousness."

Q gave Picard a smile that chilled the captain's blood. "You should," he said.

Chapter Three

"REG?" DEANNA ASKED BETWEEN two claps of thunder. "Are you feeling all right?"

Riker glanced over his shoulder at Barclay, who was manning the primary aft science station. The nervous lieutenant was looking a bit green, possibly from the constant shaking caused by the assault of the Calamarain. Despite the best efforts of the *Enterprise*'s inertial dampers, the bridge continued to lurch from side to side, a far cry from the usual smooth ride. The rocking sensation reminded Riker of an Alaskan fishing vessel he'd served on as a teen, but surely it wasn't bad enough to make anyone nauseous, was it?

Barclay started to reply, then clapped both hands over his mouth. Riker rolled his eyes and hoped the queasy crewman would not have to bolt for the crew head. Barclay was a good man, but sometimes Riker wondered how he ever got through the Starfleet screening process. Behind the command area, Baeta Leyoro snorted disdainfully.

"That will be enough, Lieutenant," Riker instructed her. Maintaining morale under such arduous conditions was hard enough without the crew sniping at each other, even if he half sympathized with the security chief's response. "How are our shields holding up?"

"Sixteen percent and sinking," Leyoro responded. She glared at the tempest upon the viewscreen.

Riker nodded grimly. They needed to find some way to retaliate. He would have preferred a more peaceful resolution to this conflict, but they were rapidly running out of options. Unfortunately, conventional weapons had thus far proven ineffective against their attacker; phasers had not discouraged the Calamarain, whose close quarters to the *Enterprise* precluded the use of quantum torpedoes. Maybe, he mused, the Calamarain required a more specialized deterrent.

Lightning flashed across the viewscreen, and an unusually violent shock wave rocked the bridge, interrupting Riker's thoughts and slamming him into the back of the captain's chair. His jaw snapped shut so suddenly he narrowly avoided biting off the tip of his tongue. To his left, he heard Deanna gasp in alarm, but whether she was reacting to the sudden impact or the Calamarain's inflamed emotions he couldn't begin to guess. At the conn, Ensign Clarze stabbed at his controls in a desperate effort to stabilize their flight but met with only mixed results. The floor beneath Riker's feet pitched and yawed like a shuttle going through an unstable wormhole. Even Data had to strain to keep his balance, digging his fingertips into the armrests of his chair. *We can't take much more of this,* he thought.

As if to prove the point, Riker felt his stomach turn over abruptly. *Oh, no,* he thought. He identified the sensation at once, even before he spotted a puddle of spilled coolant, released during an earlier impact, lifting off from the floor and floating through the air, forming an oily globule only a few meters away. "We have lost gravity generation throughout decks one through fourteen of the saucer section," Data confirmed.

At least we didn't lose the entire network, Riker thought. The ship's internal gravitation system was divided into five overlapping regions; from the sound of it, they had lost gravity in about half of the saucer. In theory, the entire battle section of the ship, including engineering, still had gravity, but for how much longer? This latest technical mishap provided an eloquent testament to the Calamarain's offensive capabilities. It took a lot to take out the gravity generators; even with a total power loss, the superconducting stators that were the heart of the graviton generators were supposed to keep spinning for up to six hours. He couldn't remember the last time he had experienced zero gravity anywhere aboard the *Enterprise,* except in the holodecks, where reduced gravity was sometimes employed for recreational purposes.

Starfleet training included zero-G exercises, of course, but Riker could only hope that the rest of the crew didn't feel as rusty as he did. The last time he'd actually done without gravity had been during his short-lived flight on Zefram Cochrane's *Phoenix,* and that had hardly been a combat situation, at least from his perspective. Even the most primitive shuttle had come equipped with its own gravity for the last hundred years or so. *We're not used to this anymore,* he worried, wishing he'd scheduled more zero-G drills before now.

Still, the bridge crew did their best to adjust to the new conditions. Keeping a watchful eye on the drifting coolant, Clarze ducked his hairless dome out of its way. Deanna's hair, already shaken loose by the previous jolts, snaked Medusa-like about her face, obscuring her vision, until she neatly tucked the errant strands back into place. Behind and above the command area, a scowling Baeta Leyoro had lost contact with the floor and begun floating toward the ceiling. Executing an impressive backward somersault, she grabbed the top of the tactical podium with both hands, then pulled her body downward until she was once more correctly oriented above the floor. "Get me some gravity boots," she snapped at the nearest security officer, who rushed to fulfill the command.

Following standard procedure, Riker clicked his chair's emergency restraining belt into place, and heard Deanna doing the same. The hovering blob of spilled coolant wafted dangerously near Data's face, and Riker anticipated a gooey mess, but the air purification system caught hold of it and sucked the viscous mess into an intake valve mounted in the ceiling, just as similar valves cleared the atmosphere of the ashes and bits of debris produced by the battle. *Thank goodness something's still working right,* Riker thought. "Ensign Berglund," he addressed the young officer at the aft engineering station, "any chance we can get the gravity back on line?"

"It doesn't look good," she reported, holding on tightly to a vertical station divider with her free hand. "I'm reading a systemic failure all through the alpha network." She perused the readouts at her console avidly. "Maybe if they try reinitializing the entire system from main engineering?"

Riker shook his head. He didn't want Geordi and his people concentrating on anything except keeping the shields up and running. "Gravity is a luxury we'll just have to do without for a while." Easier said than done, he realized. Humanoid bodies were simply not designed to function without gravity, especially so suddenly; pretty soon, Barclay wouldn't be the only bridge member seasick. He tapped his combadge. "Riker to Crusher. I need a medical officer with a hypospray full of librocalozene right away."

"Affirmative," Beverly replied. She didn't ask for an explanation; Riker realized sickbay must have lost gravity as well. "Ogawa is on her way."

By foot or by flight? Riker wondered, grateful that the turbolifts did not require gravity to operate properly. "Thank you, Doctor." Glancing around the bridge, he saw that Leyoro's security team was already distributing magnetic boots from the emergency storage lockers to every crew member on the bridge, starting with those standing at the aft and perimeter stations. The Angosian lieutenant stomped her own boots loudly on the floor as she regained her footing. "Good work," he told her tersely, indicating her team's rapid deployment.

"Standard procedure," she replied, shrugging. "I figure we're better off facing these stupid BOVs with our feet firmly on the ground."

"BOVs?" Riker asked. He didn't recognize the term, presumably a bit of slang from the Tarsian War.

Leyoro flashed him a wolfish grin. "Better Off Vaporized," she said.

That might be a bit redundant in this case, he thought, considering the gaseous nature of their foes. He appreciated the sentiment, though; he was getting pretty tired of being knocked around himself. But what could you do to an enemy who had already been reduced to plasma? That was the real problem, when you got down to it. Explosions and projectiles weren't much good against an undifferentiated pile of gases. The Calamarain had already blown themselves to atoms, and it hadn't hurt them one bit.

A partial retreat was also an option, he recalled. True, they couldn't outrun the Calamarain on impulse alone—that much he knew already—but maybe they could find a nebula or an asteroid belt that might provide them with some shelter from the storm, interfere with the Calamarain's onslaught. "Mr. Clarze," he barked, raising his voice to be heard above the thunder vibrating through the walls of the starship. "Is there anything nearby that we could hide behind or within?" Such a sanctuary, he knew, would have to be within impulse range as long as their warp engines were down.

The Deltan helmsman quickly consulted the readouts on his monitor. "Nothing, sir," he reported glumly, "except the barrier, of course."

The barrier, Riker thought, sitting bolt upright in the chair. *Now, there's an idea!*

The gravity was out, his little sister was crying, and Milo Faal didn't know what to do. Ordinarily weightlessness might have been kind of fun, but not at the moment. All the loud noises and shaking had upset Kinya, and none of his usual tricks for calming her were working at all. His eyes searched the family's quarters aboard the *Enterprise* in search of something he might use to reassure the toddler or distract her, but nothing presented itself; Kinya had already rejected every toy he had replicated, even the Wind Dancer hand puppet with the wiggly ears. The discarded playthings floated like miniature dirigibles throughout the living room, propelled by the force with which Kinya hurled each of them away. Not even this miraculous sight was enough to end her tantrum. "C'mon, Kinya," the eleven-year-old boy urged the little Betazoid girl hovering in front of him, a couple centimeters above the floor. Milo himself sat cross-legged atop a durable Starfleet-issue couch, being careful not to make any sudden movements while the gravity was gone; as long as he remained at rest he hoped to stay at rest. "Don't you want to sing a song?" He launched into the first few verses of "The Laughing Vulcan and His Dog'—usually the toddler's favorite—but she refused to take the bait, instead caterwauling at the top of her lungs. Even worse than the ear-piercing vocalizations, though, were the waves of emotional distress pouring out of her, flooding Milo's empathic senses with his sisters's fear and unhappiness.

An experienced Betazoid babysitter, Milo was adept at tuning out the uncontrolled emanations of small children, but this was almost more than he could take. "Please, Kinya," he entreated the toddler, "show me what a big girl you can be."

Such appeals were usually effective, but not this time. She kicked her tiny feet against the carpet, lifting her several centimeters above the floor. Milo leaned forward carefully and tapped her on the head to halt the momentum carrying her upward.

Kinya howled so loudly that Milo was surprised the bridge wasn't calling to complain about the noise. Not that Kinya was just misbehaving; Milo could feel how frightened his sister was, and he didn't blame her one bit. To be honest, Milo was getting pretty apprehensive himself. This trip aboard the *Enterprise* was turning out to be a lot more intimidating than he had expected.

Since their father was missing, like always, and no one else would tell them what was going on, Milo had eavesdropped telepathically on the crew and found out that the *Enterprise* was engaged in battle with a dangerous alien life-form. *And I thought this trip would be dull,* Milo recalled, shaking his head. He could use a dose of healthy boredom right now.

A thick plane of transparent aluminum, mounted in the outer wall of the living room, had previously offered an eye-catching view of the stars zipping by. Now the rectangular window revealed only the ominous sight of swollen thunderclouds churning violently outside the ship. He wasn't sure, but, judging from what he had picked up from the occasional stray thoughts, it sounded like the clouds actually *were* the aliens, no matter how creepy that was to think about. The billowing vapors reminded Milo of an electrical tornado that had once frightened Milo when he was very young, during a temporary breakdown of Betazed's environmental controls. His baby sister was too small to remember that incident, but the thunder was loud and scary enough to make her cry even louder each time the clouds crashed together.

Please be quiet, he thought at the toddler. His throat was sore from emotion, so he spoke to her mind-to-mind. *Everything will be okay,* he promised, hoping he was thinking the truth. *There, there. Ssssh!*

Kinya listened a little. Her insistent bawling faded to sniffles, and Milo wiped his sister's nose with a freshly replicated handkerchief. The little girl was still scared; Milo could sense her acute anxiety, like a nagging toothache that wouldn't go away, but Kinya became semi-convinced that her big brother could protect her. Milo was both touched and terrified by the child's faith in him. It was a big responsibility, maybe bigger than he could handle.

If only Mom were here, he thought for maybe the millionth time, taking care to block his pitiful plea from the other child. But his mother was dead and nothing would ever change that, no matter how hard he wished otherwise. And his father might as well be dead, at least as far as his children were concerned.

Despite his best efforts, Kinya must have sensed his frustration. Tears streamed from a pair of large brown eyes, gliding away into the air faster than Milo could wipe them, while her face turned as red as Klingon disruptors. His sister hovered about the carpet, surrounded by all the drifting toys and treats. Kinya grabbed a model *Enterprise* by its starboard warp nacelle and began hammering the air with it, frustrated that she could no longer reach the floor with it. Tossing the toy ship aside, she snatched the Wind Dancer puppet as it came within her grasp and twisted its ears mercilessly. Kinya managed to abuse the toys without missing a note in her tearful ululations. Milo wanted to borrow two cushions from the couch to cover his own ears, but even that wouldn't have been enough to block out her outpouring of emotion. *It's not fair,* he thought angrily. *I shouldn't have to deal with all this on my own. I'm only eleven!*

Then, to his surprise and relief, he sensed his father approaching, feeling his presence in his mind only seconds before he heard his voice in the corridor outside. His father was very irate, Milo could tell, and seemed to be arguing with someone, speaking loudly enough to be heard through the closed steel door of the guest suite. Now what? he wondered.

"This is intolerable!" Lem Faal insisted as the door slid open. He was a slender, middle-aged man with receding brown hair, wearing a pale blue lab coat over a tan suit. "Starfleet Science will hear about this, I promise you that. I have colleagues on the Executive Council, including the head of the Daystrom Institute. You tell your Commander Riker that. He'll be lucky to command a garbage scow after I'm through with him!"

Milo was amazed. Ever since Mom died, his

father had been distant, distracted, and, okay, irritable sometimes, but Milo had never heard him go all Klingon at another adult like this. What could have happened to upset him like this? Looking beyond his father, he spotted a security officer standing outside the doorway, holding on to his father's arm. Both men wore standard-issue gravity boots, and Milo wondered if the gravity had gone out all over the *Enterprise.* "I'm sorry, Professor," the Earthman said, "but, for your own safety, the commander thinks it best that you remain in your quarters for the time being." Milo sensed a degree of impatience within the officer, as if he had already explained his position several times before.

"But my work," Faal protested as the officer firmly but gently guided him into the living quarters. Milo hopped off the couch and launched himself toward his father for a closer look at what was going on. "You have to let me go to Engineering. It's vital that I complete the preparations for my experiment. All my research depends on it. My life's work!"

Because of his illness, Faal looked much frailer than his years would suggest. His whole body trembled as he railed against the unfortunate guard. Nearing the doorway, Milo slowed his flight by bouncing back and forth between facing walls. He winced every time he heard his father wheeze; each breath squeaked out of his disease-ravaged lungs.

"Maybe later," the officer hedged, although Milo could tell, as his father surely could, that it wasn't going to happen. The guard let go of Faal's arm and stepped back into the corridor. "There are extra boots in the emergency cupboards," he said, nodding in Milo's direction. "I'll be out here if you need anything," he said. "Computer, seal doorway. Security protocol gamma-one."

"So I'm under house arrest, is that it?" Faal challenged him. He grabbed the edge of the door and tried to stop it from sliding shut. "You dim-witted Pakled clone, don't you understand what is at stake? I'm on the verge of the greatest break-through since the beginning of warp travel, an evolutionary leap that will open up whole new horizons and possibilities for humanoids. And your idiotic Commander Riker is willing to sacrifice all that just because some quasi-intelligent gas cloud is making a fuss. It's insane, don't you see that?"

"I'm sorry, sir," the officer said once more, maintaining a neutral expression. "I have my orders." Faal tried to keep the door open, but his enfeebled fingers were no match against the inexorable progress of the steel door. His hands fell away as the door slid shut, shielding the unfortunate officer from further scorn.

Gasping for breath, the scientist leaned against the closed doorway, his chest heaving. His fruitless tirade had obviously cost him dearly. His face was flushed. His large brown eyes were bloodshot. He ran his hand anxiously through his hair, leaving stringy brown tufts jutting out in many different directions. Milo could feel his father's exhaustion radiating from him. Even with no gravity to fight against, it wore Milo out just watching him. "Are you all right, Dad?" he asked, even though they both knew he wasn't. "Dad?"

In a telepathic society, there was no way Milo's father could conceal his illness from his children, but he had never really spoken to them about it, either. Milo had been forced to ask the school computer about "Iverson's disease" on his own. A lot of the medical terminology had been too advanced for him, but he had understood what "incurable" meant, not to mention "terminal."

His father reached into the pocket of his lab coat and produced a loaded hypospray. With a shaky hand, he pressed the instrument against his shoulder. Milo heard a low hiss, then watched as his father's breathing grew more regular, if not terribly stronger. None of this came as a surprise to the boy; he had asked the computer about "polyadrenaline," too. He knew it only offered temporary relief from his father's symptoms.

Sometimes he wished his father had died in that accident instead of his mother, especially since Dad was dying anyway. This private thought, kept carefully locked away where no one could hear, always brought a pang of guilt, but it was too strong to be denied entirely. *It's just so unfair! Mom could have lived for years. . . .*

At the moment, though, he was simply glad to have his father back at all. "Where have you been, Dad?" he asked. He grabbed the doorframe and pulled himself downward until his feet were once more planted on the carpet. "The ship keeps getting knocked around and everything started floating and Kinya won't stop crying and I hear the ship is being attacked by aliens and we might get blown to pieces. Do you know what the aliens want? Did anyone tell you what's going on?"

"What's that?" his father replied, noticing Milo for the first time. He breathed in deeply, the air whistling in and out of his congested chest, and steadied himself. "What are you talking about?"

"The aliens!" Milo repeated. Fortunately, their father's arrival had momentarily silenced the toddler, who teetered on tiny legs before lifting off from the floor entirely. "I know it's not polite to listen in on the humans' thoughts, but the alarms were going off and the floor kept rocking and I could hear explosions or whatever going off outside and you were nowhere around and I just had to know what was happening. Have you seen the battle, Dad? Is Captain Picard winning?"

"Picard is gone," Faal said brusquely. A plush toy kitten drifted in front of his face and he irritably batted it away. "Some insignificant moron named Riker is in charge now, someone with no understanding or respect for the importance of my work." He seemed to be talking to himself more than to Milo. "How dare he try to stop me like this!

He's nothing more than a footnote in history. A flea. A speck."

This was not the kind of reassurance Milo hoped for and needed from his father. *He's worried more about his stupid experiment than us,* he realized, *same as always.* He tried to remember that his father was very sick, that he wasn't himself these days, but he couldn't help feeling resentful again. "What happened to the captain?" he asked anxiously. "Did the aliens kill him?"

"Please," his father said impatiently, dismissing Milo's questions with a wave of his hand before creeping slowly toward his own bedroom. "I can't deal with this right now," he muttered. "I need to think. There has to be something I can do, some way I can convince them. My work is too important. *Everything depends on it.* . . ."

Milo stared at this father's back in disbelief. He didn't even try to conceal his shock and sense of betrayal. How could Father just ignore him at a time like this? *Never mind me,* he thought, *what about my sister?* He looked over his shoulder at Kinya, who was watching her father's departure with wide, confused eyes. "Daddy?" she asked plaintively.

Lightning flashed right outside the living room, followed by a boom that sounded like it was coming from the very walls of the guest suite. The overhead lights flickered briefly, and Milo saw the force field reinforcing the window sparkle on and off like a toy Borg shield whose batteries were running low. The momentary darkness panicked the toddler. Tears streaming from her eyes and trailing behind her like the tail of a comet, Kinya bounced after her father, arms outstretched and beseeching. *I know how she feels,* Milo thought, breathing a sigh of relief as Faal grudgingly plucked the tearful girl from the air. "About time," Milo murmured, not caring whether his father heard him or not.

But instead of clasping Kinya to his chest, the scientist kept the whimpering child at arm's length as he handed Kinya over to Milo, who was momentarily surprised by how weightless she felt. "By the Chalice," his father wheezed in an exasperated tone, "can't you handle this?" The model *Enterprise* cruised past his head, provoking a disgusted scowl. "And do something about these blasted toys. This is ridiculous." He glanced over Milo at the tempest beyond the transparent window. "They're just clouds. How can clouds ruin all my plans?" he mumbled to himself before disappearing into his private bedchamber. An interior doorway slid shut, cutting him off from his children

The total absence of gravity did nothing to diminish the anger and disillusionment that crashed down on Milo in the wake of his father's retreat. Without warning, he found himself stuck with a semi-hysterical sibling and a murderous rage he could scarcely contain. *No,* he thought emphatically. *You can't do this. I won't let you.*

Summoning up as much psychic energy as he

could muster, he willed his thoughts through the closed door and straight into his father's skull. *Help us, please,* he demanded, determined to break through the man's detachment. *You can't ignore us anymore.*

For one brief instant, Milo sensed a tremor of remorse and regret within Lem Faal's mind; then, so quickly that it was over even before Milo realized what had happened, an overpowering burst of psychic force shoved him roughly out of his father's consciousness. Mental walls, more impervious than the duranium door sealing Faal's bedroom, thudded into place between Milo and his father, shutting him out completely.

Unable to comprehend what had just occurred, Kinya blubbered against her brother's chest while, biting down on his lower lip, Milo fought back tears of his own. *I hate you,* he thought at his father, heedless of who else might hear him. *I don't care if you're dying, I hate you forever.*

On the bridge, six levels away, Deanna Troi felt a sudden chill, and an unaccountable certainty that something very precious had just broken beyond repair.

Still looking slightly green, Lieutenant Barclay nevertheless stood by his post at the science station. His long face pale and clammy, he awkwardly clambered into the magnetic boots he found waiting there. Judging from his miserable expression, the only good thing about the total absence of gravity upon the bridge was that it couldn't possibly make him any sicker.

Riker barely noticed Barclay's distress, his attention consumed by the daring but risky stratagem that had just presented itself to his imagination. "Mr. Data," he asked urgently, "if we did enter the galactic barrier, what are the odds the Calamarain would follow us?"

"Will!" Deanna whispered to him, alarmed. "Surely you're not thinking . . ." Her words trailed off as she spotted the resolute look on Riker's face and the daredevil gleam in his eyes. "Are you sure this is wise?"

Maybe not wise, but necessary, he thought. The Calamarain were literally shaking the *Enterprise* apart; the failure of the gravity generators was only the latest symptom of the beating they had been taking ever since the cloud-creatures first attacked. Even if Data managed to invent some ingenious new way of fighting back against the Calamarain, they would never be able to implement it without some sort of respite. At that very moment, an ear-shattering crash of thunder buffeted the ship, tossing the bridge from side to side with whiplash intensity. Duranium flooring buckled and a fountain of white-hot sparks erupted only a few centimeters from Riker's boots. Feeling the heat upon his legs, he drew back his feet instinctively even as a security officer, Caitlin Plummer, hurried to douse the blaze with a handheld extinguisher.

Startled cries and exclamations reached Riker's ears as similar fires broke out around the bridge. With only one foot securely embedded in his gravity boots, Barclay hopped backward as his science console spewed a cascade of orange and golden sparks. His shoulder bumped into Lieutenant Leyoro, who drove him away with a fierce stare that seemed to frighten him even more than the flames. "E-excuse me," he stammered. "I'll just stand over here if you don't mind. . . ."

Despite the tumult, Data promptly responded to Riker's query. "Without a better understanding of the Calamarain's psychology, I cannot accurately predict their behavior should we penetrate the barrier."

Of course, Riker reprimanded himself, *I should have guessed as much.* "What about us? How long could we last in there?"

Data replied so calmly that Riker would have bet a stack of gold-pressed latinum that the android had deactivated his emotion chip for the duration of the crisis. "With our shields already failing, I cannot guarantee that the ship would survive at all once we passed beyond the event horizon of the barrier. Furthermore, even if the *Enterprise* withstood the physical pressures of the barrier, the overwhelming psychic energies at work within it would surely pose a hazard to the entire crew."

"What about Professor Faal's plan?" he asked, grasping at straws. "Can we try opening up an artificial wormhole through the barrier, maybe use that as an escape route?" It would be ironic, Riker thought, if Faal's experiment, the very thing that had ignited this crisis, proved to be their ultimate salvation. Still, he was more than willing to let Faal have the last laugh if it meant preserving the *Enterprise*. Lord knows he didn't have any better ideas.

Data dashed his hopes, meager as they were. "The professor's theory and technology remain untested," he reminded Riker. "Furthermore, to initiate the wormhole it would be necessary to launch the modified torpedo containing the professor's magneton pulse emitter into the barrier, but there is a ninety-eight-point-six-four percent probability that the Calamarain would destroy any torpedo we launch before it could reach the barrier." Data cocked his head as he gave the matter further thought. "In any event, even if we could successfully implement the experiment, there is no logical reason why the Calamarain could not simply follow the *Enterprise* through the wormhole."

Damn, Riker thought, discouraged by Data's cold assessment of his desperate scheme. The first officer was willing to gamble with the ship's safety if necessary, but there was no point in committing suicide, which seemed to be what Data thought of Riker's plan. *Never mind the wormhole*, he railed inwardly, *I should have tried entering the barrier earlier, when our shields were in better shape*. But how could he have known just how bad things would get? Why wouldn't the Calamarain listen to reason?

Turbolift doors slid open and Alyssa Ogawa rushed onto the bridge, a full medkit trailing behind her like a balloon on a leash. Gravity boots kept her rooted to the floor. "Reporting as ordered, sir," she said to Riker.

"Thank you, Nurse," he answered. "Please give everyone on the bridge, except Mr. Data, of course, a dose of librocalozene to head off any zero-G sickness." He glanced behind him where Barclay was still keeping a safe distance from both the smoking science console and Lieutenant Leyoro. "You can start with Mr. Barclay."

"Ummm, I'm allergic to librocalozene," Barclay whimpered, clutching his stomach. "Do you have isomethozine instead?

Ogawa nodded and adjusted the hypospray.

Riker repressed a groan. He didn't have time to deal with this. "Do Ensign Clarze next," he advised Ogawa. The last thing he needed was a queasy navigator. As the nurse went to work, he returned his attention to Data.

"One further consideration regarding the barrier," the android added. "Starfleet records indicate that the danger posed by the barrier's psychic component increases proportionally to the telepathic abilities of certain humanoid species." He looked pointedly at Troi. "Please forgive me,

Counselor. I do not mean to alarm you, but it is important that Commander Riker fully comprehend what is at risk."

"I understand, Data," she said, not entirely concealing the anxiety in her voice.

So do I, Riker thought. If he did dare to brave to barrier, Deanna would almost surely be the first casualty. *Not to mention Professor Faal and his children,* he realized. They were from Betazed, too, and, being fully Betazoid, even more telepathically gifted than Deanna. Flying into the barrier would surely doom the children. Could he actually give that command, even to save the rest of the crew?

"Do whatever you have to, Will," Deanna urged him. "Don't worry about me."

How can I not? he asked her silently, already dreading the pain of her loss. But Deanna was a Starfleet officer. In theory, she risked her life every time they encountered a new life-form or phenomenon. He couldn't let his personal feelings influence his decision. *If only I could switch off my own emotion chip,* he thought.

"Shields down to twelve percent," Leyoro announced. She didn't remind Riker that time was running out. She didn't need to. Working briskly and efficiently, Ogawa pressed her hypospray against Leyoro's upper arm, then moved on to Deanna. Riker hoped she wasn't wasting her time; if their shields collapsed entirely, they'd all have a lot more to worry about than a touch of space sickness. *Too bad we can't inoculate the crew against a tachyon barrage.*

Frustration gnawed at his guts. "Blast it," he cursed. "We can't stay here and we can't risk the barrier. So what in blazes are we supposed to do?"

To his surprise, a tremulous voice piped up. "Excuse me, Commander," Barclay said, "but I may have an idea."

Chapter Four

"I DON'T UNDERSTAND," THE YOUNG Q SAID. "What are we doing back here? I mean, it's a fascinating site, but I thought you'd seen enough of it."

Looking on, quite unseen, Picard wondered the same. He found himself once more facing the legendary alien artifact known as the Guardian of Forever, as did 0 and young Q. The immeasurably ancient stone portal looked exactly as it had the first time Q had brought him here: a rough-hewn torus, standing five meters high at its peak and surrounded by crumbling ruins of vaguely Grecian design. It was through this portal, he recalled, that the young Q had first drawn 0 into reality as Picard knew it.

"Never again my plans gone astray,
Never again my life locked away,

Never again to die,
Never again, say I. . . ."

0 sang softly to himself in a voice little more than a whisper; the song seemed to have special meaning to him. Could it refer, Picard wondered, to the recent debacle with the Coulalakritous? The stranger's archaic garments, he observed, no longer bore the scars of that confrontation. 0 limped across the rubble-strewn wasteland until he was directly in front of the Guardian. "Listen to me, you decrepit doorway," he addressed it, placing his hands upon his hips and striking a defiant pose. The shifting winds blew swirls of gritty powder around his ankles. "I'm not fond of you and I know you don't approve of me, but you're in no position to be picky about whom you choose to serve. I'm stronger now than when last we met, and getting more like my old self with every tick of the clock." He bent over and lifted a fist-sized chunk of dusty marble from the ground, then held it out before him. The solid marble burst into flames upon his palm, but 0 did not flinch from the fiery display, continuing to hold the burning marble until it was completely incinerated. When nothing was left but a handful of smoking ashes, he flung the smoldering residue onto the ground between him and the portal. "I trust we understand each other."

"I COMPREHEND YOUR MEANING," the

Guardian said, its stentorian voice echoing off the fallen marble columns and shattered temples around it. "WHAT AND WHERE DO YOU DESIRE TO BEHOLD?"

0 glanced back at the young Q, who sat upon a set of cracked granite steps several meters behind his companion, looking confused but intrigued. "I knew I could make this antiquated archway see reason," he told Q with a conspiratorial wink, "and the question's not where, but whom." Turning back toward the portal, he opened his mouth again, but what next emerged from his lips bore no resemblance to any language Picard had ever heard, with or without access to a Universal Translator. Indeed, he didn't seem to *hear* the words so much as he felt them seeping into his skin, burrowing directly into some primordial back chamber of his brain. He looked away from 0, back at Q's earlier self, and saw that the youth appeared just as baffled as Picard.

"What sort of language is that?" Picard asked the older Q standing beside him. He placed his hands over his ears, but the sounds—or whatever they were—still penetrated his mind. "What is he saying?"

Q shrugged. "I didn't know then," he said in a fatalistic tone, "and I don't know now. A call to arms, I imagine, or maybe just a list of names and addresses." He leaned against a tilted marble column and shook his head sadly. "What's important is, they heard him."

"Who?" Picard demanded, shouting in hopes of drowning out the unsettling effect of 0's inhuman ululation. It didn't work, but Q managed to hear him anyway.

"Them," he said venomously. He pointed past the imperious figure of 0 to the open portal itself. As before, a thick white mist began to stream from the top of the archway, spilling over onto the arid ground at 0's feet. Peering through the haze, Picard saw a procession of historical images rushing before his eyes like a holonovel on fast-forward. The races and cultures depicted were unfamiliar to him, and Picard was extraordinarily well versed in the history of much of the Alpha Quadrant, but, as one image gave way to another at frightening speed, he thought he could begin to discern a recurring theme:

Larval invertebrates emerge from silken cocoons and proceed to devour their insectile parents. Adolescent humanoids, covered in downy chartreuse feathers, riot in the streets of an elegant and sophisticated metropolis, toppling avian idols and putting ancient aeries to the torch. A lunar colony declares its independence, unleashing a devastating salvo of nuclear missiles against its homeworld.

Generational conflict, Picard realized, seizing on the common thread. *The new violently destroying the old.*

0 stretched out his hand toward the portal, beckoning with his fingers, and a figure emerged

from the haze, stepping out from the parade of matricidal and patricidal horrors to assume form and definition outside the portal. He was a silver-haired humanoid of angelic demeanor, resplendent in shimmering amethyst robes that billowed about him from the neck down. A sea-green aura surrounded him, blurring his features somewhat, and, despite his humanoid mien, he failed to achieve any true solidity, resembling a glimmering mirage more than an actual being of flesh and blood. He did not look particularly dangerous, but Picard suspected that first impressions might be deceptive, especially where any confederate of 0's was concerned.

"Gorgan, my old friend," 0 greeted him, lapsing into conventional speech. "It's been too long."

"Longer for you, I suspect, than for any other." Gorgan's deep voice echoed strangely among the barren ruins, sounding artificially amplified. He tipped his head deferentially, revealing an immaculate silver mane that swept back and away from his broad, expansive brow. Beneath the greenish glow, his face seemed pinkish in hue. "I am at your service, my liege."

0 accepted the other's expression of fealty without question. "We have plenty to discuss, but stand aside now while I round up more of our comrades from departed days."

Gorgan stepped away from the portal, seemingly content to await 0's convenience, but the young Q was incapable of such patience. "Wait just one nanosecond," he called out, springing up from the battered stone steps. "I'm not so sure about this. I agreed to accept responsibility for you, not . . . whoever this is." He gestured toward Gorgan, who regarded him with what looked like wry amusement. The newcomer's apparent lack of concern about Q's identity and objections only rankled the youth further. "I insist you tell me what in the Continuum you think you're doing."

"I'm not thinking anything," 0 said brusquely. "I'm doing it, and never mind the Continuum." He reached out once more for the portal and there was a momentary flicker within its aperture as the Guardian appeared to shift its focus. A flustered Q, having clearly lost control of the situation, stumbled hesitantly toward 0. Despite his evident unease, he also appeared consumed by curiosity. "Don't worry so much," 0 reassured him. "I promise you won't be bored."

"You can say that again," the older Q remarked gloomily.

Visions from the past or future cascaded beneath the arch of the Guardian, capturing the attention of both the young Q and Picard. Although Gorgan's face remained benignly serene, an avid gleam crept into his eyes as he watched the historical vistas unfold:

Tribes of fur-clad savages hurl rocks and sharpened bones at each other amid a primeval forest.

Mighty armies clash on battlegrounds awash in turquoise blood, the ring of metal against metal echoing alongside the cries of the wounded and the dying. A fleet of sailing ships sinks beneath the waves of an alien sea, their wooden masts and hulls torn asunder by blazing fireballs flung by catapults upon the shore. Mechanized steel dreadnoughts roll through the blasted rubble of an embattled city while bombs fall like poisonous spores from the smoke-choked sky, blooming into flowery displays of red-orange conflagration. In the hazardous confines of a teeming asteroid belt, daring star pilots flying sleek one-man vessels wage a nerve-wracking, hyperkinetic, deep-space dogfight, executing impossible turns as they fire coruscating blasts of pure destructive energy at enemy spacecraft performing equally risky maneuvers; the eternal night of space lights up like the dawn for a fraction of a second every time a sizzling beam strikes home or a brazenly fragile ship collides with an asteroid that got too close.

Picard had no difficulty identifying the theme of this grisly pageant. *War,* he realized, appalled by the sheer bloody waste of it all even as he was struck by the foolhardy courage of the combatants. *War, pure and simple.*

Called forth from the billowing fog, another entity emerged from the time portal. Even more so than Gorgan, however, this being lacked (or perhaps declined) human form, manifesting as a flickering sphere of crimson energy spinning fiercely about two meters above the ground, casting a faint red radiance on the dust and debris below. No sound emerged from the sphere, nor did its passage produce so much as a breeze to rustle the gritty powder it glided over. Whatever this entity was, it seemed even more immaterial than the gaseous Coulalakritous, consisting like Gorgan of undiluted energy, not matter at all. *Much like the energy being who impregnated Deanna Troi several years ago,* Picard recalled, *or perhaps the entity who possessed me during the Antican-Selay peace negotiations.* Indeed, Starfleet had discovered so many noncorporeal life-forms over the last couple centuries that Picard sometimes wondered if sentient energy was actually as common throughout the galaxy as organic life had proven to be. Judging from their appearance, both Gorgan and this new entity provided support for such a supposition.

"Hello again, (*)," 0 said to the shimmering sphere, and Picard hoped he would never need to pronounce that name himself, if that was in fact what the energy creature was called. "Welcome to a whole new arena, billions upon billions of new worlds, all waiting for us."

If (*) responded to 0, it did not do so in any form Picard could hear. Instead it simply spun silently in the air, undisturbed by the errant gusts of wind that blew perpetually throughout the ruins. Moving away from the Guardian, it passed straight

through a solid marble column, emerging un-
changed from the other side of the truncated
masonry. Perhaps at 0's direction, it joined Gorgan
at the sidelines, hovering a few centimeters above
the robed man's head. The crimson glow of (*)
overlapped with the other's greenish aura, yielding
a zone of brown shadows between them.

Stalled halfway between the steps and 0, the
young Q inspected the rotating sphere with interest, then remembered his doubts about this entire
procedure. "See here, 0, I can't just stand by while
you conduct all this . . . unauthorized immigration. I don't know a thing about these entities
you're so blithely importing into my multiverse."
He strode forward and laid a restraining hand upon
0's shoulder. "Can't you at least tell me what this is
all about?"

"All in good time," 0 said gruffly. Looking back
over his shoulder, he glowered at Q with enough
menace to make the younger being withdraw his
hand and step backward involuntarily. Q gulped
nervously, his eyes wide and uncertain. His gaze
fixed on his would-be mentor, he failed to notice
Gorgan and (*) advancing on him with deliberate,
predatory intent. A cruel smile appeared on the
humanoid's lips while the glowing sphere rotated
faster in anticipation. Gorgan's features shifted
behind his luminous aura, growing subtly more
bestial. The threat of violence, metaphysical or
otherwise, hung over the scene, although Picard
could not tell how much the young Q was aware of

his present jeopardy. All his anxious wariness seemed directed at 0 and what he might do next. Picard found himself in the odd position of sympathizing with Q, even though, intellectually, he recognized that the young Q could not possibly suffer irreparable harm at this point in history since he had to survive long enough to afflict Picard in the future. *Unless,* he reluctantly acknowledged, *Q is about to throw another blasted time paradox at me.*

To Picard's surprise, and the young Q's relief, 0 abruptly switched modes, adopting a more congenial attitude. His eyes no longer intimidated and his voice grew more ingratiating. Temporarily turning his back on the Guardian, he strove to allay Q's reservations while, unseen by Q, Gorgan and (*) quietly retreated to their earlier posts. "Unauthorized immigration? Really, Q, that doesn't sound like you. You weren't so cautious and conservative when you rescued me from that loathsome limbo, or when you so eloquently argued my case before the Continuum. As I recall, you stated pretty boldly that the Continuum could use some fresh blood and new ideas. Well, here they are," he said, an arm sweeping out to indicate (*) and Gorgan. "Don't tell me you've changed your mind now."

"Well, no. Not exactly," Q replied. He glanced over at Gorgan, who graced him with a beatific smile entirely unlike the one he had affected while stalking Q from behind. "It's just that this is somewhat more than I had in mind."

"You wanted the unknown," 0 reminded him. "You wanted to have an impact on the universe, bring about something new."

"Yes, but . . ." Q stammered. "These beings . . . who are they exactly? What do they want?"

"To help us, of course," 0 asserted, "in our grand and glorious campaign to elevate the standards of sentient life throughout this galaxy. What else?" He beamed at the specter and the sphere lurking on the periphery of the discussion. "I know these faithful fellows from days gone by and can vouch for them wholeheartedly. That must be good enough to overcome any dismal doubts you might have? After all, you vouched for me."

"I suppose," Q said dubiously. He looked from 0 to the mysterious pair and back again, perhaps realizing for the first time that he was distinctly outnumbered. He sighed and squinted at the fog streaming out of the time portal. "But how much new blood exactly were you planning to extract from that thing?"

"Just one more old acquaintance," 0 promised, grinning at Q's gradual acquiescence. "Then, trust me, we'll have all the support we need to embark on any crusade we choose . . . for the good of this entire reality, naturally." He called upon the newcomers to back up his claim. "Isn't that so, fellows? You're with us through thick and thin, aren't you?"

"Absolutely," Gorgan purred. Something about

his manner brought an old phrase to Picard's mind: First thing we do, let's kill all the lawyers. "I look forward to continuing our work in this brave new dimension, as I also anticipate getting to know this fine young entity."

His bodiless cohort merely hung in the air, its crimson radiance pulsing like a heartbeat. Picard found it hurt his eyes to stare at (*) for too long. *That's enough to give one a headache,* he thought. Not a pleasant prospect, this far from sickbay.

"You know," the older Q commented. "I never did warm to those two, especially that sanguinary fellow spinning like a pinwheel over there. No sense of subtlety whatsoever. You should have seen what a slaughterhouse he made of Cheron later on."

Cheron? Picard vaguely remembered an ancient civilization that was supposed to have destroyed itself via racial warfare some fifty thousand years before his own century. Was Q implying that this extradimensional visitor would eventually be responsible for the extinction of an entire species?

"Of course, I still run into them now and again," Q continued. "Now, *that's* awkward, I must tell you. Of course, they usually have the sense to go scurrying off into some miserable, insignificant corner of the cosmos whenever they sense me drawing near. And good riddance, I say."

"What are you saying, Q?" Picard asked, disturbed by the implications of Q's remarks. "That these beings still exist in our own era?"

"Your own era," Q corrected him archly. "I refuse to be tied down to any specific time or place, present attire notwithstanding." He tugged on the gray jacket of his imitation Starfleet uniform, straightening its lines. "Besides, let's not get too far ahead of ourselves, shall we? We can handle the historical footnotes later. There is still more to be seen here," he instructed Picard. "Behold."

Now flanked by Gorgan and (*), Q's younger self stood by helplessly, torn between anxiety and anticipation, as 0 advanced on the Guardian for what he had vowed would be the last time. Once more that eldritch keening flowed from 0's mouth, invoking another cavalcade of frightful images within the open maw of the portal:

An untamed tornado ravages a cultivated landscape, destroying vast orchards of alien fruit and tossing dome-shaped farms and storage facilities into the fevered sky along with the graceful reptiles who tended to the land. An earthquake rips through the heart of a populous community, the tremors opening up gaping chasms that swallow up entire parks and buildings. A majestic chain of volcanos erupts after centuries of dormancy, spewing ash and fire into the heavens and spilling torrents of plutonic lava onto half a continent, instantly reducing a thriving nation, thick with citizenry, into a smoking wasteland. Oceans of water pour from enormous clouds as a flood of biblical proportions sweeps over one unfortunate world; the deluge swiftly drowns every living thing that walked or crawled or slithered upon the surface, the evolution of millennia lost beneath the swelling sea.

These were no mere rebellions or self-inflicted wars, Picard recognized, not simply conflicts between sentient and sentient, but unequal struggles pitting mortal beings against the awesome power of nature at its most destructive. Unprovoked catastrophes: what ancient historians and jurists once labeled "acts of God."

With eerie appropriateness, what came next through the portal was nothing less than a veritable pillar of fire. Composed entirely of dancing scarlet flames, it snaked horizontally through the steaming gateway, then rose upward like a rearing serpent to achieve a height of over fifty meters above the desolate ruins. Picard felt the heat of the blazing column upon his face and he had to tilt his head back to spy the apex of the looming inferno, which he estimated to be at least two meters in diameter. Was this colossal torch truly an intelligent entity like the others Q had drawn from the portal? he wondered. It was hard to see it as anything other than an incredible thermal phenomenon, but Picard guessed that was not the case.

"As you have summoned Me, so have I come," the tower of flame proclaimed, confirming the captain's assumption. Its voice was nearly as sonorous as the Guardian's, although a touch more human in tone, having a firm yet paternal quality. "Let worlds without number prepare for My Judgment and tremble at My Wrath."

0 laughed out loud at the flaming column's words. "You don't need to put on such lofty airs on my account. I've known you too long for that." He strolled casually around the circumference of the pillar, heedless of the blistering heat radiating from it, clucking at its awesome dimensions. "Maybe you could see your way clear to taking on a more . . . approachable appearance." He shook his head wearily. "It's like talking to a bloody forest fire."

"Let it be as you request," the tower answered, sounding slightly miffed. "Many are My Faces. As numerous as the stars are the manifestations of My Glory."

"Someone thinks highly of himself," the older Q said snidely. "Or should that be Himself?"

Picard was too engrossed by the fiery pillar's sudden transformation to acknowledge Q's remark. Before his gaping eyes, the huge column of swirling flame contracted into the shape of a man, then rapidly cooled to the consistency of human flesh. The newborn figure stood a few centimeters taller than 0 and was sheathed in gleaming armor of solid gold. His stern features were adorned by a flowing, snow-white beard; Picard found himself reminded of face of Michelangelo's famous portrait of Moses, and was momentarily disappointed that He wasn't actually carrying two inscribed stone tablets. The thought occurred to him that such Old Testament imagery, including the pillar of fire itself, still lay countless aeons in the future. "Q—" he began.

The elder Q held up his palm. "Before you ask . . . no, this is not how I, as a Q, perceived 0's motley band of recruits. Instead this is how they would appear—and will appear—to humanoids such as yourself, according to your own rudimentary senses."

I suspected as much, Picard thought. As the young Q approached the forbidding new arrival, the captain wished he could fully understand how this latest visitor appeared to Q's earlier self. *If only I could see through Q's metaphors to what is actually happening.*

"Excuse me," young Q said to the armor-clad stranger. "Who are you?"

"I am The One," He replied, His arms crossed stiffly atop His chest.

"The One?" inquired Q, who was after all only *a* Q.

"He invented monotheism," 0 explained with a shrug. "Indulge Him." He raised his voice to address the entire gathering. "Old friends and comrades, call me 0 now, for I've put the pitfalls and purgatory of the past behind me. I offer you an opportunity to do the same. There are dazzling days ahead, I promise you!" Throwing an arm over

Q's shoulder, he spun the youth around so hard that the toes of Q's boots were dragged through the dust and debris. "Now let me introduce to you our proud patron, as well as our native guide to these parts, my good friend and rescuer . . . Q."

The three from the portal spread out around Q and 0, then drew in closer, surrounding the young Q, who, from where Picard was standing, seemed to be not so much basking in the attention as trying with visible effort to maintain a cocky and confident air despite the fact that, 0's flattery notwithstanding, he had rather quickly gone from being 0's all-knowing host and chaperon to ending up as the newest and junior member of a well-established group where everyone knew each other, and their actual agenda, much better than he did. "So," he said breezily, ducking out from under 0's arm while trying to slip unobtrusively out between Gorgan and The One, "how long have you fellows known 0?"

"Long enough," Gorgan asserted, pressing in upon Q and blocking his escape. The more Picard listened to it, the more Gorgan's voice seemed to be generated artificially rather than through the normal action of lungs and vocal cords. The shimmering stranger was only simulating humanity, and not entirely successfully. "Long enough to know where our best interests lie. And yours."

"Be strong in My Ways," The One added, "and you will shall surely prosper. Falter, and your days shall be filled with sorrow." He laid his hand upon Q's shoulder, and the young godling flinched instinctively, stumbling backward into the hovering presence of (*). His body fell *through* the glowing sphere, receiving what looked like some manner of jolt or chill. Emerging behind (*), Q gasped and continued to fall until he landed in a sitting position upon the ground, his limbs trembling and his eyes and mouth wide open. The palpitations quickly subsided, but Q's expression remained dazed.

"Watch yourself," 0 warned him. He took Q by the hand and helped him to his feet. His associates kept their distance this time, granting the jittery Q a bit more personal space. "There's nothing to be skittish about. We're all on the same side here." The deep lines carved into 0's weathered visage stretched to accommodate his toothy grin. "Stick with us, Q, and we'll have a fine time, you'll see. This great, gorgeous galaxy will never be the same."

"Skittish? Me?" Q said loudly, pulling together a semblance of self-assurance. "I'm nothing of the sort." He brushed the clingy dust from his trousers with elaborate indifference. "I'm simply unaccustomed to so much like-minded company. I've always been something of a lone wolf within the Continuum."

"And a black sheep, too, I think," 0 surmised. "No use denying it; it's as obvious as the smug somnambulism of the other Q. Well, you're not alone anymore, my friend. Rest assured, you're one of us now."

"Lucky me," the older Q observed from within the shadow of a tilted Doric column.

"Fallen in with a bad crowd, have we?" Picard said. He shook his head, feeling a tad disillusioned that the errors of Q's youth would prove to be so mundane. "It's an old story, Q."

"Older than you know," Q stated, "and more serious than you can possibly imagine."

How so? Picard wondered. Examining the scene, he noted that, beyond the congregation of superbeings, the Guardian of Forever had fallen still and silent. The last thin ribbons of mist dissipated into the atmosphere of the lonely setting while the empty aperture at the center of the Guardian offered only a view of the fallen temples on the other side of the portal. It appeared that whatever intelligence inhabited the Guardian had taken 0 at his word that there would be no further corridors opened between this reality and whatever distant realm 0 and his cohorts originated from. Just as well, Picard concluded. Judging from the older Q's ominous remarks, these four would prove dangerous enough.

He peered at the new arrivals. Something about them, particularly Gorgan, struck a chord in his memory, but one he couldn't quite place. He felt certain that he had never personally encountered any of these entities before, but perhaps he had reviewed some record of their existence. The buried memory teased him, and he wished he had immediate access to the *Enterprise*'s memory banks. Perhaps something from Starfleet records, maybe even from the logs of one or more of the earlier *Starships Enterprise.* "Gorgan," he muttered. "Where have I heard that name before?"

"Stardate 5029.5," Q volunteered helpfully. "In and around the planet Triacus. Before your time, of course, but I believe one of your predecessors had an unpleasant encounter with the ever-insinuating Gorgan. One James T. Kirk, to be exact." Q rested his chin upon the knuckles of one hand, striking a meditative pose. "Speaking of which, one of these days I really should go back a generation or so before your birth and see if Starfleet captains were always as humorless as you are."

Don't even think about it, Picard thought vehemently. Kirk and his crew had run into enough challenges during their long careers without the added aggravation of coping with Q. Meanwhile, he searched his memory for details regarding the original *Enterprise*'s contact with Gorgan. He dimly recalled several incidents in which Kirk's crew faced powerful beings along the lines of Q and 0. Was Gorgan the one who hijacked the *Enterprise* using some brainwashed children, or the one who turned out to be Jack the Ripper? Given the rampant generational strife in the images preceding Gorgan's entrance, he guessed the former.

"What about that one?" Picard asked, pointing

to the spinning globe of crimson light. He asked partly out of curiosity, partly to distract Q from his alarming notion of visiting the twenty-third century.

"I believe your Starfleet database refers to it as the 'Beta XII-A entity,' named for the rather forgettable world where your kind first made its acquaintance." Q scowled at the shining energy creature. "A deceptively innocuous name, in my opinion, for so bloody-minded a presence."

Beta XII-A, Picard memorized dutifully. That, too, sounded familiar, although Starfleet had charted too many planets for him to pinpoint its location and history immediately, not without Data's total recall. He resolved to research the matter thoroughly if and when Q deigned to return him to the *Enterprise.* "And what of the final entity?" he asked Q. "The one who calls himself The One?"

Q rolled his eyes. "What do I look like, an information booth? All will become clear in time, Jean-Luc. Rather than subject me to this plodding interrogation, you would do better to observe what transpires *now.*" He diverted Picard's attention back to the curious assemblage several meters away.

0 had just finished recounting his and Q's recent altercation with the Coulalakritous to Gorgan and the others. "Looking back," he admitted, "we should have started off with a more underdeveloped breed of subjects, the sort less capable of

violating the spirit of the test." He paced back and forth through the broken masonry, dragging his bad leg behind him. "Yes, that's the idea. We need to be more selective next time. Choose just the right specimens. Advanced enough to be interesting, naturally, but not evolved enough to skew the learning curve." He stopped in front of the young Q and eyed his designated host and guardian expectantly. "This is your neck of the woods, my boy. Any likely candidates come to mind?"

Q looked grateful to occupy center stage again. The one advantage he had over the others was his superior knowledge of this particular reality. "Let me think," he said, scrunching up his face in concentration. His foot tapped impatiently in the dusty gravel as he looked inward for the answer. A second later, his face lighted up as an idea occurred to him; Picard half expected a lightbulb to literally materialize over the young Q's head, but, to his relief, no such absurdity occurred. "There's always the Tkon Empire," he suggested.

Picard could not have been more startled if the young Q had suddenly proposed a three-week debauch on Risa. *The Tkon Empire,* he thought numbly, transfixed by shock and a growing sense of horror. *Oh, my God. . . .*

Chapter Five

"COME AGAIN?" RIKER ASKED.

"It's true," Barclay insisted. "I examined the probe that we sent toward the galactic barrier, the one we transported back to the ship after the Calamarain attacked, and I discovered that the bio-gel paks in the probe had absorbed some psychokinetic energy from the barrier itself, partially protecting them from the Calamarain's tachyon bursts." He waved a tricorder in Riker's face, a little too close for comfort. "It's all here. I was going to report back to Mr. La Forge about what I found, but then Professor Faal insisted on coming to the bridge, and I had to follow him, and then you assigned me to the science station after Ensign Schultz was injured—"

Riker held up a hand to halt the uncontrolled

flood of words pouring from Barclay's mouth. Sometimes, in his own way, the hapless officer could be just as long-winded as Data used to be, and as slow to come to the point. Riker took the tricorder from Barclay and handed it off to Data for analysis. "Slow down," he ordered. "How can this help us now?"

He wasn't just being impatient; with the Calamarain pounding on the ship and their shields in danger of collapsing, Riker couldn't afford to waste a moment. To be honest, he had completely forgotten about that probe until Barclay mentioned it, and he still wasn't sure what relevance it had to their present circumstances. As far as he was concerned, their entire mission concerning the galactic barrier had already been scrapped. His only goal now was to keep both the ship and the crew intact for a few more hours.

"The *Enterprise-E* has the new bio-gel paks, too," Barclay explained, "running through the entire computer processing system, which is directly linked to the tactical deflector system." He leaned against the back of the captain's chair and closed his eyes for a moment. Riker guessed that the lack of gravity upon the bridge was not helping Barclay's shaky stomach any.

"Sit down," he suggested, indicating the empty seat where the first officer usually sat when he wasn't filling in for the captain. Barclay sank gratefully into the chair, his magnetic boots clanging against the floor as he moved. "All this bio-organic technology is still pretty new to me," Riker admitted. The first Starfleet vessel to employ the new organic computer systems, he recalled, had been the ill-fated *U.S.S. Voyager,* now stranded somewhere in the Delta Quadrant. Hardly the most promising of pedigrees, even though its bio-gel paks were hardly responsible for *Voyager*'s predicament. "What does this have to do with current situation?"

"Oh, the bio-gel is wonderful stuff," Barclay declared, scientific enthusiasm overcoming nausea for the moment, "several orders of magnitude faster than the old synthetic subprocessors, and easier to replace." Riker sensed a lecture coming on, but Barclay caught himself in time and cut to the chase. "Anyway, if the ship's bio-gel paks absorb enough psychokinetic energy from the barrier, maybe we can divert that energy to the deflectors to protect us from barrier itself. In effect, we could use part of the galactic barrier's own power to maintain our shields. Like a fire wall, sort of. It's the perfect solution!"

"Maybe," Riker said, not yet convinced. The *Enterprise* was a lot bigger and more complicated than a simple probe. Besides, if any crew member was going to pull a high-tech rabbit out of his or her hat, Riker would have frankly preferred someone besides Reginald Barclay. *No offense,* he thought, *but where cutting-edge science is concerned I have a lot more faith in Data or Geordi.* He turned toward Data. "Is this doable?" he asked the android.

"The data Lieutenant Barclay has recorded is quite provocative," Data reported. "There are too many variables to guarantee success, but it is a workable hypothesis."

"Excuse me, Commander," Alyssa Ogawa said as she came up beside him. Riker felt the press of a hypospray against his forearm, followed by the distinctive tingle of medicinal infusion. Even though he had not suffered any negative effects from the zero gravity yet, he derived a twinge of relief from the procedure. One less thing to worry about, he thought.

"Shields down to ten percent," Baeta Leyoro stated, continuing her countdown toward doom. A rumble of thunder and a flash of electrical fire accented her warning. The jolt shook the tricorder free from Data's grip and the instrument began to float toward the ceiling. Data reached for the tricorder, but its momentum had already carried the tricorder beyond his reach. "Hang on," Leyoro said, plucking her combadge from her chest. She hurled the badge like a discus and it spun through the air until it collided with the airborne tricorder. The force of the collision sent both objects ricocheting backward toward their respective points of origin. Leyoro snatched the badge out of the air even as the tricorder soared back toward Data's waiting fingers. "Just a little trick I picked up on Lunar V," she said, referring to the penal colony where she and the other Angosian veterans had once been incarcerated.

Remind me not to play racquetball with her, Riker thought. *Or a game of dom-jot, for that matter.*

"Sir, we're sitting ducks here," she said. "We have to *do* something, and fast."

Riker made his decision. "Let's risk it," he declared, rising from the captain's chair. "Data, you and Barclay do whatever's necessary to set up the power feed between the bio-gel paks and the deflectors. Contact Geordi; I want his input, too. See what he can do from Engineering. His control panels may be in better shape than ours. Ensign Clarze, set course for the galactic barrier."

"Yes, sir!" the young crewman affirmed, sounding eager to try anything that might liberate them from the Calamarain. *I know how you feel,* Riker thought.

He cast an anxious look at Troi, seated to his left. "Deanna, I want you and every other telepath aboard under medical supervision before we get too near the barrier. Report to sickbay immediately and remind Dr. Crusher of the potential psychic hazards of the barrier. Nurse Ogawa, you can accompany her." He tapped his combadge. "Riker to Security, escort Professor Faal and his entire family to sickbay at once." He almost added "red alert," then remembered that the ship had been on red alert status ever since the Calamarain first appeared on their sensors. *Too bad we don't have an even higher level of emergency readiness,* he thought, *specifically for those occasions when we jump from the frying pan into the fire.*

Riker's eyes met Deanna's just as she and Ogawa entered the turbolift. For an instant, he almost thought he could hear her voice in his mind, through the special bond they had always shared. *Take care,* her eyes entreated, then the turbolift doors slid shut and she was gone.

Good enough, he thought, turning his attention back to the task before him. There had never been any need for grand farewells between them. Each of them already knew that should anything happen to either one, the other would always remember what had existed between them. They were *imzadi,* after all.

On the viewscreen, Riker caught a glimpse of starlight as the prow of the *Enterprise* pierced the outer boundaries of the Calamarain. He felt surprisingly heartened by the sight of ordinary space after long hours spent in the opaque and angry fog. Then the front of the gigantic plasma cloud overtook them, snatching away that peek at the stars. "The Calamarain are pursuing us," Leyoro stated.

"Can we shake them?" he asked.

"Not at this rate," Clarze called back from the conn. "I'm at full impulse already."

No surprise there, Riker observed. *We already knew they were fast.* "Very well, then," he said defiantly, determined to bolster the crew's morale. "Let them come along with us. I want to know just how far they're willing to take this."

With any luck, he thought mordantly, *they're not half as crazy as we are.* With all eyes glued to viewscreen, watching for the first light of the barrier as the starship zoomed head on for the absolute edge of the galaxy, Riker inconspicuously crossed his fingers and hoped for the best. *I can't believe I'm really staking the* Enterprise *on some far-fetched scheme from Reg Barclay, of all people!* This was not one of Barclay's holodeck fantasies, this was real life, about as real as it gets.

And, possibly, real death as well.

"But this isn't the way to Engineering!" Lem Faal gasped.

"I told you, sir, you and your family have been ordered to sickbay." The security officer, Ensign Daniels, kept a firm grip on the scientist's arm as he herded Faal and the children through the corridors of the starship. Milo clomped down the weightless halls in magnetic boots several sizes too large for him, cradling Kinya in his arms. He sensed that the large human crewman was rapidly losing patience with the boy's father. "Please hurry, sir. Commander Riker's orders."

Milo hurried after the two adults. His father struggled to free his arm from Daniels's grip as, wheezing with every breath, he tried to convince the crewman to let him go to Engineering instead. *What was he planning to do with us,* Milo wondered bitterly, *just dump us on the poor ensign or drag us along to his shipboard laboratory?* Probably the former, he guessed. Two children would just be in the way in Engineering, the same as they always seemed to be in the way where their father was concerned. Resentment seethed in the pit of his stomach. Concern for their future, and anxiety over their safety, only slightly diluted the bile that bubbled and boiled within him every time he thought of his father's gross abandonment of them. *Even now,* he brooded sullenly, *he's more worried about his precious apparatus than us.*

Red-alert lights flashed at every intersection, emphasizing the urgency of their fast-paced march through the *Enterprise.* Ensign Daniels didn't know or wouldn't explain why they had to go to sickbay in such a rush, but obviously it was some sort of emergency. *Are they expecting us to get sick? Are the aliens winning the fight? Are we going to die?* Milo gulped loudly, imagining the worst, but tried not to look afraid in front of his little sister. He had to act brave now, for her sake, even though his whole body trembled as he visualized a dozen different ways for the cloud-monsters to kill him. *What if we have to evacuate the ship?* The galactic barrier, he knew, was a long way away from the nearest Federation colony. *Will the clouds let us escape in peace?*

At least Kinya was weightless, too. Even still, his arms were getting tired from holding Kinya this whole hike and his legs weren't feeling much better.

It still takes effort to move this much mass, he realized. "Are we almost there?" he asked Ensign Daniels. His voice only cracked a little.

"Almost," the security officer promised. They rounded a corner and Milo saw a pair of double doors on the left side of hall. A limping crewman, a Tellarite from the look of him, staggered toward the doors from the other end of the corridor, clutching a wounded arm against his chest. Blood leaked from a cut on his forehead and scorch marks blackened the sleeves of his uniform. One tusk was chipped, and his hoof-shaped boots clicked at an irregular pace against the steel floor. A rush of pain from the injured officer hit Milo before he had a chance to block it. His hands stung vicariously from the man's burns. He felt a phantom ache where his tusk would have been had he been a Tellarite. He closed his eyes and pushed the stinging sensations away.

Kinya, who had been sobbing and squirming as Milo carried her, fell still at the sight of the wounded crewman. She tightened her grip on his shoulders. The Tellarite really looked like he'd been through a war. Even Milo's father was quieted, at least for the moment, by this open evidence of the battle being waged, his indignant remarks to Ensign Daniels trailing off in mid-insult. Seeing his father act so subdued and reasonable, Milo had to wonder how long it would last. Not long enough, he guessed.

The double doors opened automatically at the

Tellarite's approach, offering Milo his first look at sickbay. His instant impression was one of crowded, constant activity. Between the wounded and those treating them, there had to be over a dozen people in the medical facility, many of them strapped onto biobeds whose monitor screens reported on the vital signs of each patient. Despite the packed conditions, however, everything seemed to be under control. The activity was fast, but not frenzied; health workers in magnetic boots shouted queries and instructions to each other, but nobody was panicking. Sickbay worked like a machine, with a dozen moving pieces working in perfect coordination with each other. Polished steel instruments flew from hand to waiting hand. Ensigns with handheld suction devices efficiently cleared the atmosphere of floating fluids, ash, and fragments of cloth. Was it always so busy, he wondered, or only during emergencies?

The doors stayed open for Milo and his party. Ensign Daniels led the way and gestured for the rest of them to follow. Remembering the pain he had absorbed from the Tellarite, Milo clamped his mental shields down hard before stepping inside.

The air had a medicinal odor that he had learned to associate with sterilization fields, and the overhead lights were brighter than elsewhere on the ship. They made their way carefully into a hive of ceaseless motion that adjusted to their presence and flowed around them as easily as a mountain stream circumvents the rocks and other obstacles in its path. A levitating stretcher bumped into Milo's shoulders and he caught an alarming glimpse of a severed antennae taped to the stretcher next to the unconscious body of a wounded Andorian crew member. *Can they reattach that?* he wondered, turning around quickly so that his sister wouldn't see the grisly sight. He heard a frightened whimper from the little girl.

The doctor attending to the Andorian, a tall man with a bald dome, glanced down at the children and rolled his eyes. "Marvelous," he muttered sarcastically. "Children, no less. We'll be getting cats and dogs next." Curiously, Milo did not detect irritation from the man, or any other emotion; it was almost like he wasn't really there.

Looking around, Ensign Daniels spotted Dr. Crusher deeper inside the facility, directing her medical team like a general on a battlefield. "Doctor!" he called out, weaving through the throng. "I have Professor Faal and his family."

A nurse rushed up and handed Dr. Crusher a padd. A report on one of the patients, Milo assumed. She glanced at it quickly, tapped in a few modifications, then handed it back to the nurse, who hurried away to see to the doctor's instructions. Dr. Crusher took a deep breath before focusing on the security officer and his charges. "Good," she said. "I've been expecting them." She nodded at Milo's father. "Give me just a second, Professor, then follow me." Her sea-green eyes surveyed the room. "Alyssa, take over triage until I get back.

Make sure the EMH looks at those radiation blisters on Lieutenant Goldschlager, and tell Counselor Troi to join me as soon as she finishes up with Cadet Arwen." She took custody of Faal's arm from the security officer. "Thank you, Ensign. If you're not needed elsewhere, we can really use an extra pair of hands. Contact Supply and tell them to beam another load of zero-G plasma infusion units directly to sickbay. We can't replicate them fast enough."

"Yes, Doctor," Daniels promised. "First thing."

"Come with me, Professor," the doctor said, leading them away from the main crush of the medical emergency ward to an adjacent facility, where they found a row of child-sized biobeds as well as what looked like a high-tech incubator unit. The pediatric ward, Milo realized unhappily. He felt like a patient already and he hadn't even been injured yet. "Here, let me help you with her," Dr. Crusher said to him, bending over to lift Kinya from his grateful arm, which he stretched until its circulation returned. Kinya squalled at first, but the doctor patted her on the back until she got used to her new address. "That's a good girl," she cooed, then wiped her own forehead with her free hand. "Thank you for coming, Professor. We're in a crisis situation here, obviously, but I want to make sure you and your family are properly cared for."

"Never mind that," Faal said. His face looked flushed and feverish. The effects of weightlessness, Milo wondered, or something more serious?

"What's this all about, Doctor? I demand an explanation."

Dr. Crusher glanced down at Milo, then decided to choose her words carefully. "To elude the Calamarain, Commander Riker has decided to take the *Enterprise* into the outer fringe of the barrier. He believes that our engineers have devised a way to provide us with some protection from the barrier, but it seemed wisest to place all telepaths under direct medical observation." She nodded toward the listening children. "I don't think I need to explain why."

She didn't need to. Milo knew how dangerous the galactic barrier could be, especially to anyone with a high psionic potential; just because he resented his father's work didn't mean he hadn't paid attention to what his parents had hoped to accomplish. Even humans, who were barely telepathic at all by Betazoid standards, sometimes had their brains fried by the barrier, and now the *Enterprise* was taking them right into it! Milo shuddered at the thought. The battle with the clouds—with the *Calamarain,* he corrected himself—had to be going badly if Commander Riker was desperate enough to fly into the barrier instead. *We should have never left Betazed,* he thought. *We're all going to die!*

His father sounded just as upset by this turn of events, although for different reasons. "But he can't," he exclaimed, "not without my wormhole." His chest heaving, he leaned against the central incubator and groped for his hypospray. "That's the whole point. That's why we're here."

"Right now Commander Riker is primarily concerned with the safety of the ship," another voice intruded. Milo sensed Counselor Troi's arrival even before he saw her framed in the entrance to the kid's ward. She walked toward the other two adults, taking care to step around Milo. "I can assure you, Professor, that the commander has considered every possibility, including your wormhole theory, and he truly believes that he is acting in the best interests of everyone aboard, including your children."

"But he's not a scientist," Faal wheezed. The hypospray hissed as it delivered a fresh dose of polyadrenaline to his weakened body. "What does he know about the barrier and the preternatural energies that sustain it?"

The counselor tried her best to calm him. "Commander Riker may not have specialized in the hard sciences, and certainly not to the extent you have, but he's consulted with some of our best people, including Commander La Forge, and he and Lieutenant Commander Data and Lieutenant Barclay feel tha—"

"Barclay?" Faal exploded, his voice sounding perceptibly stronger than seconds ago, and Milo felt Troi's heart sink. He didn't know who Barclay was, but the counselor instantly realized that she had made a mistake in mentioning his name. "Do you mean to tell me that my own extensive research into the barrier and its effects is being trumped by the scientific expertise of that clownish incompetent? By the Holy Rings, I've never heard such lunacy."

"Please, Professor," Dr. Crusher said firmly. "There is no time to debate this. The decision has been made and I need to prepare you and your family before it's too late." She gestured toward one of the kid-sized biobeds. "What I'd like to do is set our cortical stimulators on a negative frequency in order to lower the brain activity of you and the children to a more or less comatose state during the period in which we are exposed to the psionic energy of the barrier. The same for you, Deanna," she added. "Along with the extra shielding devised by . . . Data and Geordi . . . that should be enough to protect all of you from any telepathic side effects."

She sounded very certain, but Milo could tell she wasn't nearly as confident as she pretended to be. Didn't she know she couldn't fool a Betazoid? Maybe the doctor and the counselor should actually listen to his father. Despite his failings as a parent, Milo figured his father probably knew more about the barrier than anyone in the Federation.

Lem Faal sure thought so. "This is so ridiculous I can't even begin to describe how insane it is," he insisted, returning his hypospray to the inner pocket of his jacket. "It was bad enough when Riker just wanted to retreat from the barrier, but to go forward into it without even attempting my experiment . . ."

"Perhaps you should worry less about your experiment and more about your children," the doctor said heatedly. Milo sensed her anger at his father's skewed priorities. She lowered Kinya onto one of the miniature biobeds. His sister sat sideways on the bed, her small legs dangling over the edge. "According to Starfleet conventions, I don't require your consent to protect your family during a red alert, but I do expect your cooperation. Deanna, please escort the professor back to the adult ward. Have Nurse Ogawa find biobeds for both you and Professor Faal. I'll be with you in a few minutes, after I've prepared the children."

Counselor Troi laid her hand on the man's arm, but Milo's father had exhausted his patience as well. He reached out unexpectedly and snatched Dr. Crusher's combadge off her lab jacket. "Mr. La Forge," he barked, speaking into the shiny reflective badge, "this is Lem Faal. Generate the tensor matrix at once and prepare to launch the magneton generator. This is our last chance!"

Geordi's voice emerged from the badge, sounding understandably confused. "Professor Faal? What are you doing on the comm? Has Commander Riker authorized this?"

"Geordi, don't listen to him!" Dr. Crusher tried to grab the badge back from Faal, but the obsessed scientist batted her hand away impatiently.

"Forget about Commander Riker," he shouted, the badge only centimeters away from his face. Saliva sprayed from his lips.

"We're so close, we have to try it. Anything else would be insane."

"You're out of line, Professor," Geordi told him emphatically, "and I'm busy. La Forge out."

"No!" he shouted into the badge, even though the connection had already been broken off. "Fire the torpedo, blast you. You have to fire the torpedo!"

A hyprospray hissed as Dr. Crusher applied the instrument to his left shoulder. "Dad!" Milo cried out as his father stiffened in surprise. His face went slack as his eyelids drooped and he sagged backward into the doctor's waiting arms.

"Don't worry," she assured Milo. "I just prescribed him an emergency tranquilizer. He'll be fine later." With the counselor's help, she guided his father's limp body out of the pediatric ward into primary facility. An Octonoid crewman with both his lower arms in slings hopped off a biobed to make room for Faal.

Despite the narcotic, the scientist's anxiety did not abate entirely. Although his eyes remained shut, his lips kept moving, driven by a powerful sense of urgency that not even the tranquilizer could quell. Standing next to the biobed, his ears turned toward the unconscious man, Milo could barely make out his father's delirious whispers.

"Help me . . . we're so close . . . you can't let them stop me . . . please help me."

Who is he talking to? Milo wondered. *Me?* "I don't know how to help you, Dad. I don't know what I can do."

"You mustn't blame yourself for any of this, Milo," Counselor Troi told him, placing a comforting hand upon his shoulder. He could sense her sincerity and concern, as well as an underlying apprehension concerning Lem Faal. "Your father has simply been under a lot of stress lately."

That's one way of putting it, he thought, some of his resentment seeping through. He wondered if the counselor, who was only half Betazoid, could tell how angry he got at his father sometimes.

"We should hurry," Dr. Crusher said, interrupting his moment with the counselor. She glanced at Lem Faal's sleeping form and breathed a sigh of relief. "I want to get the children put under first," she explained to Troi, "then I can look after you and Professor Faal."

Unsure what else to do, Milo followed the two women back into the pediatric ward, where he watched Dr. Crusher tend to Kinya. His little sister squirmed and cried at first—watching her father collapse had upset her once again—but the doctor put her to sleep with a sedative, then stretched the toddler out on the biobed. Retrieving a pair of compact metallic objects from a pocket in her lab coat, she affixed the shiny gadgets to Kinya's small forehead. "These are only cortical stimulators," she told Milo while simultaneously checking the readings on the display panel mounted above the bed. Milo didn't know what she was looking for, but she appeared satisfied with the readings. "They won't hurt her, I promise."

"I know," Milo said. "I believe you." In some ways, Dr. Crusher reminded him of his mother. They both always seemed to know what they were doing, and they didn't talk down to him. He appreciated that.

"Too bad Selar transferred to the *Excalibur*," she commented to Troi as she made a final adjustment to the devices attached to Kinya's head. "Vulcans are supposed to be resistant to the barrier's effects, despite their telepathic gifts. No one really knows why, although there are any number of theories."

Milo was too worried about everything else to get interested in how Vulcan brains worked. At the doctor's direction, he climbed onto the empty bed across from Kinya's. From where he was sitting, he could see his father sleeping in the next ward over. To his surprise, he saw his father's face twitching, the fingers of his hand flexing spasmodically. Lem Faal looked like he was waking from a nightmare. *How long is that tranquilizer supposed to keep him down anyway,* Milo wondered, *and should I alert the doctor and the others?*

Counselor Troi must have sensed his uncertainty because she turned and followed his gaze to where his father rested fitfully. Her eyes widened as Faal's entire body convulsed, then sat up suddenly. Running his hand through his disordered hair, he shot darting glances around the sickbay like a hunted animal searching desperately for an escape route. His bloodshot eyes were haunted and a thin string of saliva dribbled from his lower lip. Milo scarcely recognized his father.

"Beverly!" Troi called out, attracting the doctor's attention. The counselor rushed toward the open doorway between her and the adult ward. "Please, Professor, you have to stay where you are. We're getting closer to the barrier. The doctor has to prepare you."

At her mention of the barrier, Faal's wild eyes filled with purpose. Gasping for breath, he lowered himself off the bed and started to stagger across the crowded sickbay toward the exit. Caught up in their own emergencies, the various nurses and patients paid little attention to the gaunt, determined-looking Betazoid making his way through the maze of bodies and medical equipment. Milo hopped off his own bed and hurried after Troi, watching her pursue his father. "Milo, wait!" Dr. Crusher called to him, but he didn't listen to her.

Younger and healthier than the dying scientist, Counselor Troi quickly caught up with Faal and grabbed his elbow from behind. "You have to stay here," she repeated urgently. "You're not safe."

Faal spun around with a snarl, a glint of silver metal flashing between his fingers. Milo recognized the object immediately: his father's ubiquitous hypospray, loaded with polyadrenaline.

No, Milo thought, disbelieving. *He wouldn't!*

But he did. Amid all the noise and activity, he couldn't hear the hypospray hiss when his father pressed it against her throat, but he saw her mouth open wide in surprise, watched her face go pale. It happened so fast there was nothing anyone could do to stop him. She clutched her neck instinctively, releasing her hold on Faal, and swayed dizzily from side to side, her gravity boots still glued to the duranium floor. She started hyperventilating as the polyadrenaline hit her system, huffing rapidly in short, ragged breaths. Her eyes glazed over and the veins in her throat throbbed at a frightening pace. Milo guessed that her heart, her lungs, and her entire metabolism had gone into overdrive, burning themselves out. She was swaying so wildly that she surely would have hit the floor if not for the absence of gravity.

"Deanna!" Dr. Crusher shouted. To Milo's relief, the doctor shoved her way past him to attend to her friend. Taking Troi's pulse with one hand, she immediately administered some sort of counteragent via her own hypospray. The antidote took effect almost instantly; Milo was glad to see Troi's breathing begin to slow. She looked like she was stabilizing now, thanks to Dr. Crusher's prompt response. *Praise the Holy Rings,* Milo thought, grateful that his father had not actually killed the counselor.

Lem Faal had not lingered to view the consequences of his actions, or to wait for a security officer to show up. Peering through the bustle of sickbay, Milo spotted his father disappearing through the double doors that led to the corridor outside. Milo chased after him, his oversized boots slowing him down more than he liked. Still occupied with the stricken counselor, Dr. Crusher did nothing to stop him from threading his way toward the exit. The doors swished open in front of him and he was free of sickbay when an unexpected hand grabbed onto his collar, dragging him back into the ward. "And where do you think you are going, young man?" a voice said sternly.

It was the bald-headed doctor, the one who didn't register on Milo's empathic senses. He eyed Milo dubiously, keeping a firm hold on the boy's collar. "I'm afraid no one is released from sickbay until they've been given a clean bill of health by a qualified health care professional."

"But my father!" Milo said, looking frantically at the exit as the doors slid shut again.

"First things first," the doctor insisted. "We'll deal with your father's appalling breach of protocol later. First we need to return you to the pediatric ward."

Milo had a vision of cortical stimulators being applied to his forehead and tried to free himself from the doctor's grip. *What's going to happen to my dad if I'm out cold?* All the doctors and nurses were too busy to bring his father back to sickbay before the ship entered the barrier. *It's up to me to save Dad,* Milo thought. "Let me go!" he yelled, but the bald doctor only tightened his grip. He was surprisingly strong.

"No!" Dr. Crusher ordered the other physician. With one arm wrapped around Counselor Troi to steady her, the ship's chief medical officer had clearly taken notice of Milo's near escape. "Don't let him get away," she instructed her colleague.

"I wouldn't dream of it," he replied archly, "even if my behavioral parameters included dreaming." Milo wasn't sure what he meant by that, but the doctor sure wasn't letting go of him anytime soon. He was about to give up when the whole sickbay shook like a malfunctioning turbo-lift. *The cloud monsters,* Milo guessed. *They must be trying to stop the* Enterprise *from going into the barrier.*

"Crusher to Security," the doctor said, tapping the badge on her chest. Obviously, she intended to send Security after Milo's father. The badge emitted a high-pitched whine, however, which was clearly not what Dr. Crusher had expected. "What the devil? There's something wrong with the comm system."

The overhead lights flickered and, to Milo's surprise, so did the doctor holding his collar. *He's a hologram,* the boy realized, taking advantage of the doctor's momentary instability to break free and run for the exit. "Stop!" the hologram cried, and tried to seize Milo again, but his immaterial fingers passed uselessly through the fleeing child. "You haven't been discharged yet!" He glanced back at Dr. Crusher, then shrugged helplessly. "Don't look at me. *I'm* not responsible for unexpected power fluctuations. This is all Engineering's fault."

Milo barely heard the holo-doctor's excuses. As the sickbay doors whished shut behind him, he found himself confronted with a three-way intersection—and no sign of his father. *He can't have gone far,* he thought, silently blaming the hologram for slowing him down, *but which way did he go?* Milo searched telepathically for his father, but could not sense his presence anywhere. *He must be blocking me out,* he realized. Frustrated, he tried to guess where his father would want to go next.

Engineering, of course, and his equipment. Hadn't he tried to convince Ensign Daniels to take him to Engineering in the first place? Milo scanned the adjacent corridors for the nearest turbolift entrance, then raced down the left-hand hallway. Maybe he could still catch his father before ... what? Milo had no idea what exactly he hoped to accomplish. He only knew that he had to do *something* before his father did anything terrible to himself.

Or someone else.

Chapter Six

GLEVI UT SOV, EMPRESS OF TKON, awoke one morning in the second year of her reign, during the latter days of the Age of Xora, with a feeling of unaccountable unease. There was a wrongness afoot, if not with her, then with the empire she hoped to rule wisely and well for many decades to come. Rising to a sitting position upon the coach, propped up by numerous soft cushions, each embroidered with the sacred emblem of the Endless Flame, she listened carefully to the silence of the early morning. Had any alarm or summons disturbed her dreams, calling her to cope with one emergency or another? No, the quiet of her private chambers was quite unbroken. Nothing had roused her except her own premonitions.

Hooves pawing the ground. . . . A fragment of a

dream flashed through her memory. *Curved horns stabbing at the sky.* For an instant she could almost recall the entire dream, but then the memory slipped away, banished from her consciousness by the dawn of waking. What had she been dreaming again?

She rubbed her golden eyes with the back of her hand, wiping away the dried residue of slumber, stretched luxuriously, and deftly lowered her bare feet into a pair of fur-lined slippers resting on the floor. She could have commanded any number of attendants to help her rise and prepare for her duties, but she preferred to look after herself. Soon enough today, affairs of state would demand her attention for the remainder of her waking hours; for now, the beginning of each day remained her own.

The subdued night glow of the opaque crystal walls faded automatically as elegant chandeliers flooded the chambers with light, highlighting the intricate colored patterns of the antique Taguan carpet upon the floor. The empress paid little attention to the ornate designs of the rug, which had been in her family since her great-grandfather's time. Her shadow preceded her as she stepped away from the coach, the hem of her silk gown trailing upon the carpet. A translucent screen, upon which was printed a copper representation of the flame emblem, descended silently from the ceiling, sealing off the imperial bedchamber from the forefront of her quarters. Her desk, carved from the finest D'Arsay teak, awaited her, as did her favorite chair.

The outer rooms felt chilly this morning. "Warmer," she stated simply, "by, oh, seven and a half grades." Her technologists assured her that someday soon it would no longer be necessary to actually speak aloud to their homes and offices; the new psi-sensitive technology now being developed in labs throughout the empire would allow one to direct any and all instrumentality by thought alone. She frowned at the notion, not entirely sure she liked the idea of her palace knowing what she was thinking.

Yawning, she sat down in her chair. The room was already feeling warmer and more comfortable, but, despite the reassuring tranquillity of her chambers, she could not shake the ominous mood with which she had woken. She searched her memory, trying to bring to light any disturbing dream that might have left her spirit troubled, yet no such nightmare came to mind. As far as she recalled, her sleep had been soothing and unruffled until the very moment she came awake.

From where, then, had come this persistent sense of impending danger? "Show me the city," she said to the smooth, crystalline wall facing her and, like a window opening upon the world outside the palace, a panoramic view of a sprawling metropolis appeared on the wall, providing the empress with a live image of Ozari-thul, capital city of the great world Tkon, center of the Empire of the Endless Flame.

Resting her chin in her palm, she gazed out upon the city, her city, seeing nothing that would account for her anxious presentiments. Ozari-thul at dawn looked nearly as placid as her chambers, the vast majority of the city's twelve million inhabitants not yet stirring from their homes. Graceful towers, winding like crystal corkscrews, pierced the morning sky, while ribbons of interlocking roadways guided a few scattered vehicles on postnocturnal errands throughout the city. The blazing sun rose to the south, and she could not help noticing how much larger and redder it seemed now than it had in the not-so-long-ago days of childhood. That so swollen a sun should actually be *cooler* than it had once been struck her as paradoxical, but her scientists assured her that was indeed the case, and certainly the changing weather patterns of the last few years had borne their theories out.

Is that it? she wondered. Was her knowledge of the geriatric sun's eventual fate coloring her perceptions of the morning? That seemed unlikely. She had known about the long-term threat posed by their sun for years now, since even before she assumed the throne after her mother's death. Besides, the empire's finest scientists all agreed that the expansion of the sun, as that familiar yellow orb evolved into what the physicists called a red goliath, would not engulf the homeworld, as well as the rest of the inner planets, for several centuries. More than time enough for the Great Endeavor to come to their rescue—or was it?

She felt a stab of hunger, prompting her to ask for her breakfast, which instantly materialized on her desk: a beaker of hot tea and a plate of toasted biscuits, with *susu* jam and just a dab of imported Bajoran honey. Frankly, she would have liked more honey, but it wasn't worth the scolding she would receive from the court nutritionists, who fretted about the foreign sweeteners in the delicious amber spread. It was her duty, after all, to keep her mind and body fit, although she sometimes wondered what was the good of being empress if she couldn't even have an extra dollop of honey now and then.

A tinted crystal disk was embedded in the top of the teak desk. Washing down a tiny bite of biscuit with a sip of moderately spiced tea, she gazed at the disk and called up the most recent report on the progress of the Great Endeavor. Dates and figures scrolled past her eyes; as always, she was impressed by the sheer, unprecedented scale of the project, as well as the enormous expense. To literally move the sun itself out of the solar system, then to replace it with a younger star taken from an uninhabited system light-years away . . . had any other species *anywhere* ever attempted such a feat? Only to preserve Tkon itself, the sacred birthplace of their people, would she even dream of undertaking so colossal an enterprise. Small wonder her nerves were jittery.

And yet . . . according to this report, the Endeavor was proceeding on schedule and only slightly over budget. If necessary, she would bankrupt the imperial treasury to save the planet, but that drastic a sacrifice did not seem to be called for at present. Work was continuing apace on the solar transporter stations, their prospective new sun had not yet displayed any serious irregularities, and everything appeared to be in order. If all went according to plan, they would be ready to attempt the substitution within her lifetime. The Endeavor was no more risky today than it had been the day before, so why did she feel so perturbed?

With a word or two, she cleared the crystal viewing disk and called for her first minister. The image of an older man, seen from the waist up, appeared at once within the crystal. From the look of him, Rhosan arOx had already been at work for an hour or so. A ceremonial cloak of office was draped over his shoulders and his graying hair was neatly groomed. His cheeks had a healthy violet hue, which reassured her more than she wanted to admit. *He looks like he can manage affairs for many more years,* the empress thought, *just as he did for Mother.* "Good morning, Most Elevated," he said. "How can I help you?"

"Nothing too urgent," she replied, reluctant to burden him with her indistinct worries. "I was merely interested in . . . well, the state of the empire."

The vertical slits of his pupils widened their

golden irises. "If I may take the liberty of asking, is something troubling you, Most Elevated?"

He's still as perceptive as he ever was, she thought. "It is most likely nothing," she assured him. "I feel . . . fretful . . . this morning, for no apparent reason. The foolish fancies of an inexperienced empress, most likely."

"I doubt that," he said promptly, "but I will be happy to allay your cares by informing you what I know." His gaze dropped to the surface of his own desk; over the last several months, he had taken over an increasingly larger share of her executive duties, freeing her to concentrate on the Great Endeavor. "Let's see. Labor negotiations with the Diffractors' Guild are dragging on, the United Sons and Daughters of Bastu are protesting the latest interplanetary tariffs, the Organians turned back our envoy again, and some fool politician on one of the outer worlds—Rzom, I believe—is refusing to pay his taxes, claiming the Great Endeavor is, quote, 'a sham and a hoax,' end quote, making him redundant as well as a damn idiot." Rhosan looked up from his data display. "Just the usual headaches, in other words. Nothing that should cause you excess concern."

"I see," the empress said, her tea and biscuits getting cold. "Thank you for your concise summary of the issues at hand. I don't believe any of the matters you mentioned could be the source of my thus far baseless apprehensions. Please forgive me for disturbing your work with such a nebulous complaint."

"It was no trouble," he insisted. "I hope I was able to put your mind to rest."

"Perhaps," she said diplomatically. "In any event, you may return to your numerous other responsibilities." Governing an empire of seven trillion inhabitants was no small task, as she well knew. "I shall see you later today, at the Fathoming Ceremony."

"Until then," the first minister acknowledged, dipping his head as she closed the connection. The crystal disk went blank. *If only I could dismiss my qualms so easily,* she mused. None of the routine difficulties Rhosan had alluded to justified the sense of dread that cast an inauspicious cloud over each passing moment. She raised her teacup to her lips, hoping the warmth of the tea would dispel the chill from her soul, but knowing in her heart that there was no easy balm for the doubts and fears that afflicted her.

A design etched onto both cup and plate caught her eye. The Endless Flame, ancient symbol of the empire since time immemorial. In olden days, she recalled, now lost in the haze of myth and legend, her primal ancestors were said to have been prophets, mystics, and seers. Their visions, according to archaic lore, had proven instrumental in the founding of the dynasty. Those distant days were long departed now, and subsequent rulers had required no such oracular prowess to guide the empire, but she couldn't help wondering, amid the miraculous technology of their modern age, if the blood of seers still flowed through her veins. Would her eldest forebears have recognized this seemingly inexplicable anxiety, this puzzling tremor in her psyche and spirit?

A single shard of memory lodged in her mind, less than a heartbeat in duration. A barely recalled sliver of a dream about . . . hooves?

Something *terrible* was coming, of that she was convinced.

"Comfortable, confident, trapped by tradition, enamored of their own hallowed history, and drunk with delusions of destiny," 0 sneered at the mighty Tkon Empire. "They're perfect, Q! I couldn't have chosen any better."

Five attentive entities, plus two more whose presence was unknown to the others, watched the planet Tkon spin beneath them, no larger than a toy globe compared to the scale on which Q and the others currently manifested themselves. From their lofty vantage point, several million kilometers above the world where the young empress dwelt, they could see a swarm of satellites, artificial and otherwise, orbiting the central planet. Tkon was the fourth planet in its system, and its influence spread outward in an expanding sphere of imperial hegemony that encompassed colonies on both the inner and outer worlds of its own solar system as well as distant outposts lit by the glow of alien stars. Tkon's defenses, based on those same satellites, colonies, and outposts, were formidable enough to discourage aggression from the barbarian races who lurked beyond the outermost reaches of the empire. 0 and his cohorts, on the other hand, couldn't have cared less about Tkon's vast military resources.

"Actually," the young Q said, "I've always considered the Tkon a civilizing factor in this region of the galaxy." He was starting to regret suggesting the Tkon Empire in the first place. What kind of testing did 0 have in mind? Nothing too severe, he hoped. "Their accomplishments in the arts and sciences, although aboriginal by our standards, naturally, are laudable enough on their own terms. I'm particularly fond of the satirical profile-poems of the late Cimi era—"

"Q, Q, Q," 0 interrupted, shaking his head. "You're missing the point. It's these creatures' primitive progress that makes them the ideal test subjects for our experiments. Where's the sport in testing some backward species that can barely split an atom, let alone synthesize antimatter? That would be a total waste of our time and abilities." He scowled at the thought before turning his mind toward brighter prospects. "These Tkon, on the other hand, are just perfect. Not too primitive, not too powerful. They're hovering at the cusp of true greatness, waiting for someone like us to come along to push them to next level . . . if they're able."

"Precisely," Gorgan agreed. He licked his lips in anticipation. "I can already see some intriguing possibilities for them."

"In them," Q corrected, assuming the other was referring to the Tkon's potential as a species.

Gorgan shrugged. "As you prefer."

"They have grown overproud and must be humbled," The One pronounced. "They must drink bitter waters before they face My Judgment."

(*) merely flashed through pulsating shades of crimson, awaiting 0's command. A Tkon starship, en route to the eleventh planet in the home system with a crew complement of one thousand two hundred and five, approached the gathered immortals. Although traveling over twenty times the speed of light, it seemed to Q to be crawling toward them, and not much larger than an Organian dovebeetle. Despite, or perhaps because of, the difference in scale between the gleaming vessel and the immaterial onlookers, the ship remained unaware of Q and the others even as it came within their proximity. It glided between Q and 0, who nonchalantly reached out and swatted the miniature spacecraft away, sending it tumbling through space and into the hard red radiance of (*).

Moments later, as Q reckoned time, (*)'s influence caused a bloody mutiny to erupt aboard the ship, leading ultimately to a helix drive explosion that blossomed into a firefly flash of blue-green before dimming into nothingness. (*) glowed a little brighter afterward, savoring its snack.

It had happened so quickly, from this celestial point of reference, that Picard could scarcely keep up with all that was happening, let alone grasp its meaning. "That ship," he murmured. "All those lives . . ."

"A matter of no importance," Q insisted, "a tiny teardrop of tragedy before the deluge. You mustn't let yourself be distracted by such marginalia. The fate of an empire, and more, is at stake."

Picard nodded grimly, unable to speak. He knew full well what was coming, and Q was right: The destruction of a single starship was next to nothing compared to the apocalypse ahead.

"You have to admit," 0 said to the young Q, the tiny starship already forgotten, "the Tkon still have a long way to go before they're remotely comparable to us, or even that fetid fog we first ran into."

"I don't know," Q responded, the bright tiny spark that had been a spacecraft still imprinted on his metaphysical retinas. Intellectually, he liked the idea of helping lesser life-forms evolve; it certainly beat the unending boredom the Continuum provided in such dispiriting quantities. Primitive species had often proved more unpredictable, and therefore more entertaining, than his fellow Q . . . with the possible exception of Q herself. On the other hand, when it came to actually visiting trials and tribulations on a harmless little species like the Tkon, who had worked so hard to achieve their own modest triumphs . . . well, he found it seemed vaguely unsporting. "They seem to be doing fairly well on their own," he observed.

"Fairly well?" 0 echoed. He laughed so loud that Q found himself blushing without really knowing why. "They're nowhere close to transcending fourth-dimensional existence, let alone achieving true cosmic consciousness. Why, they still require a massive infrastructure and social hierarchy just to satisfy their crude physical needs." He rolled his eyes and raised his hands in amazement. "You can't let yourself get sentimental about your subjects, no matter how cute and comical they are. Face the facts, Q. At this rate, it will take them a couple of eternities to catch up with us, if they even last that long, which I sincerely doubt. They've gotten smug, complacent, convinced that they're sitting at the top of the evolutionary ladder. They have no more incentive to evolve further, which means they're just short of total stagnation. They need to be reminded that there are bigger forces in the universe, sublime mysteries they haven't even begun to unravel."

"So be it," The One seconded, nodding His bearded head ponderously. His golden armor clanked as He crossed His arms atop His chest, the metallic ringing resounding across five dimensional planes and creating unaccountable subspace vibrations that caused technicians to scratch their heads in confusion throughout the entire empire. "Let it be written."

"If testing these beings is indeed on the agenda," Gorgan pointed out, "we should do so swiftly." He gestured toward the flaming thermonuclear globe at the center of the Tkon's solar system. "That old sun is clearly on its last legs."

Q glanced at the orb in question, seeing at once that Gorgan was correct. The sun of Tkon, a standard yellow star of no particular distinction aside from its usefulness to the Tkon, had almost depleted its store of hydrogen atoms. Soon enough, the helium in its core would begin fusing into carbon, eventually causing the star to swell into a bloated red caricature of its former self, and, from the look of things, swallow up all of the inner planets, including Tkon. "Seems to me," he suggested, "that the Tkon have challenges enough without us adding to their difficulties."

"Which is why this is exactly the right time to test them," 0 insisted, looming over the endangered world like a constellation. "Now is the defining moment of their existence. Can they remain focused on the big picture despite their trivial everyday concerns, not to mention whatever ingenious obstacles we place before them? Will they perish with their star, abandon their homes for distant shores, or achieve the impossible in the face of impediments both natural and supernatural?" He rubbed his palms together eagerly. "It should be a fascinating experiment!"

"Er, what kind of impediments did you have in mind?" Q found himself looking backward over his shoulder, half expecting to find the entire Continuum looking on in disapproval. *If they had any idea what 0 has in mind . . . !* To his surprise, he discovered that the danger of incurring his peers' censure only made 0's plans all the more irresistible. There was an undeniable, if vaguely illicit, thrill in defying propriety this way. If only there was some way to scandalize the Q and the others without inconveniencing the Tkon too much.

"Why, whatever we feel like," 0 stated readily. Q envied his reckless, carefree attitude. "You don't want to plan these things too much beforehand. You need to leave yourself room to improvise, to invent and elaborate. It's as much an art as a science." He gestured toward the solar system at their feet. "Go ahead," he urged Q. "It was your idea. It's only fitting you take the first shot. Indulge yourself. Employ that extraordinary imagination of yours. Give their tiny, terrestrial, time-bound minds something to really think about."

Q gathered his power together, feeling the creative energies crackle in his hands. *This is it,* he thought. *This is my chance.* A peculiar sense of . . . suspense? tension? . . . percolated within him. It was a strange, but not altogether unpleasant sensation. After all this time, after countless aeons spent waiting for the opportunity to show what he could do, what if he couldn't think of anything? What if he made a mistake or, worse yet, committed some ghastly cliché that just made 0 and the rest think less of him? He felt the pressure of the others' expectant gaze, savored an unprecedented fear of failure, then took a deep if figurative breath, absorbing inspiration from the ether. "Suppose," he said tentatively, not quite committing himself, "I miraculously extended the life span of their sun by another four billion years?" Easy enough, he thought; all that was required was a fresh infusion of elemental hydrogen into the star's core. "That would come as a real stunner to them, wouldn't it? What do you think they will do with all that extra time? How will their society and institutions react? It should make for an informative experiment, don't you think?"

0 sighed and rubbed his brow wearily. Gorgan and The One shook their heads and stepped backward, placing a bit more distance between them and Q, who could tell at once that his suggestion had not been well received. *Hey, don't blame me,* he thought indignantly. *It was my first try, after all.*

"You're missing the point," 0 explained. "That's no test; that's a *gift.*" He spit out the word as if it left a bad taste in his mouth. "Four billion extra years? What's that going to teach them—or us, for that matter? Progress, even survival itself, must be earned. Challenges are to be overcome. Benevolence is for babies."

Q's ears burned. Was 0 calling him a baby? Why, he was almost seven billion years old! "Can't the unexpected come in positive forms as well as negative?" he argued. "Isn't a species' reaction to miraculous good fortune as significant, as educational and edifying, as the way they cope with adversity?"

"On some abstract, intellectual level perhaps," 0 said grudgingly, "but take it from me, Q, it's a lot more boring, for the tested and tester alike. What would you rather do, watch the Tkon cope with the ultimate issues of life or death, or simply feed them a few cosmological crumbs now and then, watching from afar as they scurry around in gratitude?" He yawned theatrically. "Frankly, I have better things to do than watch you dote on an undeserving warren of underdeveloped, overpopulated vermin. Where's the sport in that?" He paced back and forth across the sector, his footsteps creating deep impressions in the fabric of space-time that would someday be charted by the first Verathan explorers, five hundred thousand years later. "Come on, Q. Surely you can do better than that. What's it going to be?"

"I don't know," Q blurted, feeling both embarrassed and resentful. "I'm not sure." Why was 0 making this so hard? *It's not fair,* he thought. *The Continuum is forever badgering me about going too*

far; now 0 is unhappy because I won't go far enough.
He wanted to *do* something, but not necessarily *to*
anyone.

"Listen to me, Q," 0 entreated. "This is what
you've always wanted, a chance to use your innate
abilities the way they were always meant to be
used. Don't censor yourself before you even begin.
Don't hold back. Show the Tkon, and the rest of
the multiverse, what you're really made of. Put the
fear of Q into them!"

Well, not fear exactly, Q thought. Still, 0 had a
point. Realistically, there was no way to make an
impact on the universe without affecting the Tkon
or some species like them. He couldn't balk now,
not if he was really serious about joining 0 in his
campaign. Despite his qualms, he felt a tingle of
excitement, a sneaky thrill that was only heightened by the sense that he was getting away with
something he shouldn't. "All right," he declared,
"let's start with something silly and see where we
go from there."

Without warning, thousands upon thousands of
plump, juicy red *vovelles,* a Tkon fruit not unlike a
tomato, poured from the sky above the great city of
Ozari-thul. The succulent deluge pelted the streets
and rooftops of the capital, leaving a wet, pulpy
mess wherever the falling fruits came to rest. The
fruits exploded upon impact with masonry or flesh,
spraying everyone and everything with sloppy red
debris. The people of the city, the great and the
lowly alike, ran for shelter, then stared in awe and

amazement at the inexplicable phenomenon. Slitted golden eyes blinked in disbelief while psionic announcements urged the citizens to remain calm. "Not bad," 0 pronounced. "A bit adolescent, but okay for a start."

Q was delighted by the results of his opening move. He laughed out loud as a ceremonial parade down the heart of the city was reduced to pandemonium by the unnatural downpour, sending both marchers and onlookers scrambling, already dripping with raw seed and juice, slipping and sliding in the gory remains of thousands of skydiving fruits. The high priestess of the Temple of Ozari, her immaculate white robes and headdress splattered with pulp, tried futilely to finish the Ritual of Ascension until an overripe *vovelle* cut her off in the midprayer. But not everyone found the bizarre fruitfall an ordeal or an offense; small children, exhilarated by the marvelously messy miracle, ran squealing through the streets, scooping up handfuls of pulverized fruit innards to hurl at each other, giggling deliriously as the gooey redness ran through their hair and down their faces.

Q was just as gratified and amused. All that tremendous chaos, and all because of him! Whyever had he waited so long to play this game? One whimsical notion, and he had affected the lives of millions, maybe even billions, of other beings. This was a day that neither he nor the Tkon Empire would ever forget, and he was just getting warmed up. Why, he could do anything now, anything at all.

A million outrageous possibilities popped into his mind. He could bring the colorful gods and monsters of Tkon mythology to life, or make their entire history flow backward. He could imbue an ordinary Tkon with a fraction of Q-power and see what happened next, or turn himself into a Tkon for a time. He could make them speak exclusively in limericks or sign language or Ionian pentameter. He might even change the value of *pi* throughout the entire empire or lower the speed of light; just imagine the divine confusion and merriment that would ensue! The possibilities were as infinite as his imagination. He could hardly wait to get started.

But suppose he got carried away? The thought materialized within his mind as unexpectedly as the fruits bombarding Ozari-thul, surfacing from some surprising core of responsibility at the locus of being. The possibilities at hand were almost too unlimited. For the first time, Q was frightened by his own omnipotence.

The rain of *vovelles* halted abruptly, leaving a puzzled population to gaze quizzically at the now-empty sky. They peeked out nervously from beneath archways and covered pavilions, half expecting the fruits to return in greater numbers, perhaps accompanied by icemelons and *susu* as well. Automated sanitation systems began clearing away the slippery debris. Awe and wonder gave way to feverish speculation and debate as news of the bizarre incident immediately spread to every corner of the empire. Despite a full imperial investigation, however, including the subatomic and electromagnetic scrutiny of over five thousand barrels of *vovelle* pulp, plus countless hours of careful analysis and ontological theorizing, no satisfactory explanation was ever provided, nor did the empress and her people come close to guessing the truth—until much later.

"What's the matter, Q?" 0 asked. "Why have you stopped?" He must have known from the look on Q's face that the young godling was not merely gearing up for some newer and greater escapade. "Is there a problem?"

"It's nothing," Q said, unable to meet the other's eyes; he didn't want to admit to any second thoughts. What kind of rebel was he if he got squeamish about a mere harmless jest? They'd think he was a coward, afraid of upsetting the Continuum. "I was simply concerned about the long-term ecological impact of all those plummeting succulents." The excuse sounded feeble even to his own ears. "It's just that I want to pace myself, not use up all my creativity on the first evolving life-form that catches my eye."

"But you were only getting warmed up," 0 told him. "That was nothing but a schoolboy prank. Not that I don't like a good joke as much the next all-powerful life-form, but don't you want to try something, well, more serious?"

"Maybe later," Q said. It was tempting to play with the Tkon again, try out some of his new ideas, but he didn't want to be pushed into anything he was uncomfortable with by simple peer pressure alone. *If I wanted to just go along with the crowd, I could have stuck with the Continuum. I'm only going to do what I want to do—just as soon as I figure out what that is.*

"I see," 0 answered. He looked disappointed in Q, but refrained from any further criticism. "Well, why don't you sit this one out while Gorgan and the others show you how it's done." He nodded at his companions, who began to descend and disperse to the far-flung borders of the Tkon Empire, their very substance shrinking and growing more compact as they accommodated themselves to the mortal plane of their respective targets. Soon they appeared to be no larger than the individual denizens of the worlds they had each selected, but appearances, in this case, were extremely deceiving. "They'll just soften them up for us," 0 told Q. "You and I, maybe we can deliver the coup de grâce later on, after our friends have had their fun." He strolled over to Q and rested his celestial frame upon an invisible chair. "You'll like that, Q. The final test. The exam to end all exams. That's what makes it all worthwhile, you'll see."

"Really?" Q asked, too keyed up to sit. He watched the receding forms of Gorgan, (*), and The One with mixed emotions. Part of him, the part that had thoroughly enjoyed raining overripe fruit upon the palaces of Ozari-thul, wished he was going with them. Another part, from which his trepidations had emerged, waited nervously to see what sort of stunts Q's old acquaintances were intent on. "What kind of final test?" he asked.

"Later," 0 promised. "For now, just sit back and enjoy the show."

I'll try, Q thought, settling back into a comfortable curvature of space-time, adjusting the gravity until it fit just right and resting his head against a patch of condensed dark matter. He had to admit, in spite of his occasional reservations, there was something exceptionally stimulating about not knowing what was going to happen next.

Chapter Seven

GALACTIC BARRIER, HERE WE COME, Riker thought as the *Enterprise* came within sight of the perilous wall of energy. He wasn't looking forward to justifying this decision to Captain Picard, in the unlikely event that they ever met again. Two empty chairs flanked the captain's seat; with Picard away and Deanna off in sickbay, the command area felt even lonelier than usual.

"There it is," Ensign Clarze called out unnecessarily. Even through the stormy chaos of the Calamarain, the luminous presence of the barrier could be perceived, shining through the temperamental clouds like a searchlight through the mist and throwing a reddish purple radiance over the scene upon the viewer. *Let's hope that it's not luring us on to our destruction*, Riker thought. At maximum impulse, they would be within the barrier in a matter of moments.

"Steady as she goes, Mr. Clarze," he instructed. A loose isolinear chip, its casing charred by the explosion that had liberated it from a broken control panel, drifted between Riker and the viewscreen, pointedly reminding him that the gravity had gone the way of most of their shields. *Thank heaven we still have life-support,* he thought, *after the beating we've taken.* He suspected that the old *Enterprise-D,* as durable as she was, would have already succumbed to the Calamarain's assault. *We upgraded just in time.*

"Shields at eight percent," Leyoro reported. Small wonder that the ship felt like it was shaking itself apart. The Calamarain, perhaps becoming aware of Riker's desperate strategy, threw themselves against the hull and what remained of the deflectors with the same relentless ferocity they had displayed for hours now. *Don't they ever get tired,* he thought, *or is that just something we solids have to put up with?*

"Data. Barclay. Where's that extra energy?" He smacked his fist against the arm of the chair. "We need those shields."

"Scanning for it," Barclay said from the aft engineering station. Now that the pressure was on, the nervous crewman seemed to find a hidden reserve of professionalism, or maybe he was just too busy to be frightened. *This had better work,*

Riker thought, drawing comfort from the fact that Geordi had looked over Barclay's findings and seconded Data's technical evaluation of the plan. *That's as much as I can ask for, given our lousy situation.* "Yes," Barclay reported, "I think I'm reading something now. The bio-gel paks are being energized by the proximity of the barrier. I'm picking up definite traces of psionic particles."

Lightning crashed across the prow of the saucer section, and sparks spewed from the engineering station, the electrical spray gushing toward the ceiling instead of raining upon the floor as they would have under ordinary gravitational conditions. It looked like a geyser of fire. Barclay had no choice but to step back from the sparking console while he waited for the emergency circuits to shut down the geyser. "Commander," he said, chagrined, "I can't monitor the bio-gel paks anymore."

Terrific, Riker thought bitterly. "Data, take over from your station. Divert whatever energy we've absorbed to the shields immediately." *It will have to be enough.*

"Yes, Commander," Data acknowledged, his synthetic fingers flying over the control panel faster than any human eye could follow. "Initiating energy transfer now."

Here goes nothing, Riker thought. Everything depended on Barclay's wild scheme.

"Shields back up to seventy percent," Leyoro reported in surprise; Riker didn't think she was the sort to believe in miracles. "The readings are very peculiar. These aren't like any deflectors I know, but they're holding."

And just in time, Riker thought as the ship plunged into the barrier. He braced for the impact, wondering briefly if it was even possible for the ship to be knocked about more than the Calamarain had done. The light radiating from the viewer grew brighter and for an instant he believed he saw the Calamarain flash strangely, their vibrant colors reversed like a photographic negative. Then the whole screen whited out, overloaded by the incredible luminosity of the barrier. The hum of the Calamarain, and the thunder of their aggression, vanished abruptly, replaced by a sudden silence that was almost as unnerving. It was like going from a battlefield to a morgue in a single breath, and creepy as could be.

"Commander," Leyoro exulted, "the Calamarain have withdrawn. They can't stand the barrier!" She let out a high-pitched whoop that Riker assumed was some sort of Angosian victory cry. A breach of bridge protocol, but forgivable under the circumstances. He felt like cheering himself, despite the eerie quiet.

But, having shed the Calamarain at last, could they survive the barrier? He hoped that their adversaries, in choosing the better part of valor, had not proven wiser than the *Enterprise.* "Mr. Clarze," he commanded, "come to a full stop." He didn't want to go any deeper into the barrier than they had to, let alone face whatever dangers might be waiting on the other side, with the ship in the shape that it was. "Leyoro, how are our new and improved shields holding up?"

The deathly hush of the barrier had already spread to the ship; the lights of the bridge dimmed, then went out entirely, leaving only the red emergency lights and the glow from the surviving consoles to illuminate the stations around him. The familiar buzz of the bridge faded as lighted control panels flickered before falling dead. The forward viewer was useless, the screen blank. They were flying blind, more or less.

"Sufficiently, I think," Leyoro allowed. "The readings are difficult to interpret; the psychic energy bombarding the ship is the same energy that is maintaining our shields, which makes them hard to distinguish from each other."

"How much longer can we stay here?" he asked, cutting straight to the crux of the matter. He felt a dull ache beneath his forehead, and recalled that Kirk had lost close to a dozen crew members on his trip through the barrier, their brains burned out by some sort of telepathic shock. He suddenly wondered if his decade-long psychic bond with Deanna could have left him peculiarly vulnerable to the telepathic danger of the psychic energy now surrounding the ship. *Lord only knows what its doing to my frontal lobes,* he thought, *even through our shields.*

Leyoro shook her head, unable to answer his

question. Her glee over eluding the Calamarain had given way to concern over their present status. He saw her grimace in pain, then massage her forehead with her fingers. *Never mind my brain,* he thought, *what about Leyoro's?* It had not occurred to him before that her modified nervous system, permanently altered by the Angosians to increase her combat readiness, might put her at risk as well.

He looked to Barclay and Data instead. "How long?" he asked again, wondering if the real question wasn't how long they *could* stay within the barrier, but how long they dared to.

"It is impossible to state with certainty," the android informed him. "As long as the bio-gel paks continue to draw psychic power from the barrier, we should be safe, but we must allow for the possibility that these unusual energies, which the bio-gel paks were never designed to accommodate, may burn out the paks at any moment, in which case our situation would become significantly more hazardous."

"Um, what he said," Barclay confirmed, twitching nervously. Paradoxically, his self-conscious mannerisms had returned as soon as the immediate danger passed. *He works best under pressure,* Riker guessed. *The less time he has to fret about things, the better he copes.*

"Understood," he said. "Good work, both of you. Contact Commander La Forge and tell him to start repairing the damage done by the Calamarain. Top priority on the shields; with any luck, we can get our conventional deflectors up and running before these new bio-gel paks burn themselves out."

"What about the gravity, sir?" Barclay asked. Despite the anti-nausea treatment from Nurse Ogawa, he still looked a little green around the gills. Simple spacesickness, or was Barclay's cerebrum also taking a beating from the barrier? Riker recalled that the engineer's brain had been artificially enhanced once before, when the Cytherians temporarily increased his intelligence. Barclay's IQ had returned to normal eventually, but it was conceivable that he could have picked up a little heightened telepathic sensitivity in the process. *Data may be the only crew member aboard who is entirely immune to the effect of the barrier,* Riker realized.

Riker shook his head in response to Barclay's query. "Shields first, then the warp drive. We'll just have to put up with weightlessness a little longer." To keep up morale, he allowed himself an amused grin. "Think of it as a vacation from gravity."

"Now that we're free of the Calamarain's damping influence," Leyoro pointed out, "the warp engines may be operative again."

That's right, Riker thought, immediately tapping his combadge. "Geordi, we're inside the outer fringes of the barrier, but the Calamarain have retreated. What's the status of the warp engines?"

"Not good, Commander," Geordi's voice stated, exerting its own damping influence on Riker's hopes. "I don't know if it was the Calamarain or the barrier or both, but the warp nacelles have taken an awful lot of damage. It's going to take several hours to fix them."

Blast, Riker thought, not too surprised. As he recalled, the barrier had knocked out Kirk's warp engines, too, the first time he dared the barrier. Plus, when you considered all the pounding they had received from the Calamarain's thunderbolts, and with minimal shields there at the end, he figured he should be thankful that at least the comm system was working. "Go to it, Mr. La Forge. Riker out."

"It may be just as well, Commander," Data commented. "It is impossible to predict the consequences of going to warp within the barrier itself. I would be highly reluctant to attempt such an experiment without further analysis of the unknown energies that comprise the barrier."

Except that that may be a risk we have to take, Riker thought, *especially if the Calamarain are waiting for us right outside the barrier.* "What about those angry clouds we just got rid of?" he asked Leyoro. It was possible that the Calamarain, assuming the *Enterprise* destroyed by the barrier, may have left for greener pastures. "Any sign they're still hanging around out there?"

"I don't know, sir," Leyoro said unhappily; it was obvious that the security chief did not like having to keep disappointing her commander. Just as obviously, her head was still bothering her. She rubbed her right temple mechanically, while a muscle beside her left eye twitched every few seconds. "The barrier is so intense its overwhelming our sensors. They can't detect anything past it."

So we're blind, deaf, and numb, Riker concluded. The big question then was what was more dangerous, staying inside the barrier or facing the Calamarain? *We already know we can't beat the Calamarain as is,* he thought, *so our best bet is to stay put until Geordi can get the warp drive working again, then try to make a quick escape.* He surveyed the bridge, inspecting the faces of his crew, and was glad to see that all of them, including Barclay, seemed fit enough for action. He considered sending Leyoro to sickbay for a checkup, but there was a host of people aboard, all of them in danger; he couldn't afford to start relieving officers just because they might have a suspicious headache. His own head was throbbing now, but none of his people looked like they were ready to keel over.

Yet.

Chapter Eight

DURING THE FIFTH YEAR OF THE REIGN of the empress, on an unusually chilly summer night in the largest city on Rzom, the eleventh planet in the primary solar system of the Tkon Empire, a young man stood on the wide crystal steps leading to the front entrance of the imperial governor's mansion and exhorted the crowd that had gathered in the spacious and well-lit plaza to hear him speak. A life-sized statue of the empress, carved from the purest Rzom marble and posed heroically atop an elegant pedestal at the center of the plaza, looked on in silence.

"Why," he asked the onlookers rhetorically, "should we pay exorbitant taxes, wasting the resources of a lifetime, just to preserve an overcrowded old world millions of miles from here, whose time has come?"

About a third of the crowd, most the same age as the speaker, cheered his words enthusiastically, while others muttered among themselves or cast angry yellow stares at the youth upon the steps. A contingent of five safeties, clad in matching turquoise uniforms, flanked the crowd, watching carefully for the early signifiers of a brewing disturbance. The faces of the safeties were fixed and expressionless, displaying no response to the young man's fervent oratory. Pacification rings waited patiently on the fingers of each safety's hand, linked to sophisticated neutralization equipment embedded in the very walls and pavement of the city. So far, there had been no cause to employ the rings, but the safeties remained alert and ready. Nervous faces, perhaps even the governor's, peered through the curtained windows of the palace, viewing the drama from behind the safety of reinforced crystal walls.

"That world is our birthplace," a woman shouted indignantly from the forefront of the crowd. From the looks of her, she was a governmental functionary of approximately the sixth echelon, whose reddish hair was already turning silver. A disk-shaped emblem melded to the collar of her insulated winter mantle proclaimed that she had voluntarily donated more than her allotted share to the Great Endeavor.

The young man's partisans among the crowd, students mostly, greeted the woman's passionate outburst with jeers and laughter. Emboldened by their support, the speaker on the steps hooted as well. "I wasn't born there and neither were you," he shot back, winning another round of cheers from his contemporaries. Despite the chill of the evening, on a world little known for its warmth, his vermilion cloak was open to the wind and flapping above his shoulder as he spoke. His ebony locks were knotted in the latest style. "I'm proud to say that I was born here on Rzom—and to Hades with decrepit Tkon!"

Many of the older spectators clucked disapprovingly and shook their heads. "You should be ashamed of yourself," the aging functionary said. "You don't deserve the blessings of the empire!"

One crystal step above and behind the youthful firebrand, unobserved by either his supporters or detractors, nor by the watchful eyes of the vigilant safeties, Gorgan watched with pleasure as the public debate grew more heated. *It's always so easy,* he thought, *pitting the young against the old. This new plane is no different than any other realm.*

The graying woman's admonition was seconded by others in the audience. This time those rallying around her matched the volume of the young people's catcalls and derisive glee. "That's right," another man yelled. He looked like an archivist or invested myth reader. "Go live among the barbarians if that's what you want. Real Tkon know that the homeworld is worth any sacrifice."

The open show of opposition seemed to rattle the leader of the dissidents, who stepped backward involuntarily, passing effortlessly through the immaterial form of Gorgan, who casually eased to one side for a bit more personal space. The proud young Rzom faltered, momentarily at a loss for words, but Gorgan came to his rescue, whispering into the youth's ear in a voice only his unconscious mind could hear.

"Blessings? What blessings?" the speaker demanded, parroting the words that flowed so easily from Gorgan's lips. "Over fifteen percent of the empire's adult laborers are devoted to the empress's misguided Endeavor, and over twenty-seven percent of the entire imperial budget! All to keep the inner planets from meeting their natural fate. Can you imagine what else could have been done with all that time and treasure, the advances we could have achieved in art, science, medicine, exploration, and social betterment? The finest minds of a generation are being squandered on a grandiose exercise in sentimentality and nostalgia." His voice grew bolder and more confident as Gorgan fed him subliminal cues. "Our ancestors had the courage to physically leave Tkon generations ago; we should have the courage to let go of it spiritually at long last. Let's work together to enhance the future, not preserve the past!"

"Hear, hear!" cried a young woman, barely past adolescence, her emerald tresses knotted so tightly that not a single strand blew freely in the wind. "Tell them, Jenole!"

The man beside her, wearing the indigo crest of a licensed commerce artist, gave her a contemptuous sneer. "Spoiled whelp," he muttered, loud enough for her to hear. Throughout the assembled throng, individuals eyed their neighbors skeptically and began clustering into hostile pockets of two or more, placing physical as well as ideological distance between themselves and those who disagreed with them. Soon the crowd had parted into two hostile camps, glaring at each other and shouting slogans and insults at their fellow citizens. Even the acutely disciplined safeties began to let their masks of neutrality slip, betraying their inclinations and allegiances with a slightly downturned lip here, an arched eyebrow or furrowed brow there.

Marvelous, Gorgan thought, delighted to see the people turning on themselves, splitting apart along generational lines. *Just marvelous.* It was his curse and his glory that he could only achieve and wield power through the manipulation of others, but that restriction was of little import when such creatures as these proved so easy to beguile.

"And what of the trillions of inhabitants of the inner worlds?" the older woman challenged the youth. "Are you prepared to cope with the countless refugees the dying sun will send stampeding in our direction? Not to mention the loss of our history, the end of all archaeological research into the distant past, the utter destruction of sites and natural wonders hallowed by millions of years of striving and civilization?" She paused for breath, then turned around to face the divided assemblage. "Don't future generations deserve a chance to gaze upon the sacred shore of Azzapa? Or walk in the footsteps of Llaxem or Yson?" She held out her hands to the crowd, pleading for their understanding. "Don't you see? If we let Tkon and the other worlds be destroyed, then we're cutting out the very heart of the culture we all share."

Gorgan was disturbed to see uncertainty upon the faces of some of the younger members of the audience. He scowled at the aging bureaucrat whose words appeared to be striking a nerve in listeners both young and old. *She's making too much sense,* he brooded. *Something has to be done.*

Leaving the leader of the dissidents to his own devices, Gorgan glided down the steps toward the woman, the hem of his voluminous gown leaving no trail upon the polished surface of the steps. He crept silently to her side until his face was only a finger away from her ear. *You don't stand a chance,* he whispered. *You're too old. Your time has passed.*

Higher upon the crystal steps, the youth called Jenole attempted to regain the mob's attention, along with the loyalty of his followers. "Tkon's no heart. It's just a planet, a big rock in the endless null . . . like a hundred million other worlds." He thumped a fist against his chest, raising his voice to

167

heighten the impact of his impassioned declaration. "The real heart of the empire is right here! On Rzom, and inside us all!"

His fellow students cheered in unison, some of them a bit less robustly than before, drawing murderous looks from the opposing camp. The narrow gazes of the safeties arced back and forth between the students and their critics, watching both sides carefully. The silicon rings on their fingers glinted beneath the elevated lights of the plaza, which cast a gentle, faintly violet radiance over all that transpired.

"But that doesn't *mean* anything," the functionary protested, responding to Jenole's shouted claim to the heart of the empire. She tried to match his fiery intensity, but found her will and energy fading. *It's no use,* a voice at the back of her mind whispered, sounding very much like her own. *There's no point, you've already lost.* Despite several layers of insulated fabric to protect her from the winter, she felt a chill work its way into the marrow of her bones. *Tkon is doomed. Nobody cares. The sun is dying and so are you. . . .*

Still, she tried to rally her spirits, fighting against the despair and hopelessness that descended over her like a suffocating fog. "No, you don't understand. We have a choice." She could barely hear her own words over the insidious voice inside her skull *(It's a lost cause),* but she struggled to force her argument out through her lips. "We can either run from the disaster or prevent it. Diaspora or deliverance."

"What's that?" her opponent seemed to bellow at her. "Speak up. We can't hear you."

Sadness shrouded her like a heavy net, dragging her down. "What do you want?" she murmured. *There is no hope.* Her chin sagged against her chest as her gaze dropped to the uncaring steps below. *They'll never learn.* "Why won't you listen? We have a choice. It doesn't have to happen. . . ."

She receded back into the crowd, as if drawn by some inexorable gravitational force, leaving Gorgan alone and triumphant upon the lower steps. *Despair is a powerful weapon,* he gloated, *especially for those already feeling the tug of entropy upon their bodies and souls.* He contemplated the victor of the debate, standing tall before the imposing edifice behind him, blithely incognizant of the alien influences that had driven his critic from the field. *Arrogance, too, has its uses. With both tools at my disposal, I can sever any bond, tear asunder any union, and work my will on the scraps that remain.*

One of those scraps, clad in a cloak as florid as his oratory, trumpeted his cause to the entire plaza. "You see, the rightness of our position cannot be denied! Down with the musty memory of Tkon. The future belongs to the new age of Rzom!"

His peers took up his cry, but at the fringes of the crowd people began to drift away. The older citizens in particular, having lost their most vocal advocate, seemed to lose interest in the confrontation. One by one, they turned away, shrugging dismissively. It was cold out, after all, and they had better things to do. Beneath their crisp, spotless uniforms, the coiled muscles of the safeties geared down to an only slightly lessened state of readiness.

Gorgan noticed the difference and, noticing, frowned. The situation had plateaued too soon and now ran the risk of inspiring nothing more than empty rhetoric. He could not settle for mere words, no matter how inflammatory. It was time to up the stakes, accelerate the conflict to the next level. He eyed the safeties, so self-assured in their authority, and smirked in anticipation of what was to come. *You have no idea what awaits you.*

He did not need to draw any nearer to the cocksure youth standing astride the top steps to project his new suggestions into such a willing mind. He rode the momentum he had already brought about to egg the self-infatuated student leader on to greater heights of rebellion.

"Friends, allies, brothers and sisters in arms," Jenole called out, the regal facade of the governor's palace looming behind him. "Listen to me. We need to send a message to everyone who has tried to force down our throats their Great Endeavor." He spat out the name as if it were an obscenity. "To the governor, to the selfish cowards back on Tkon, and even to the empress herself."

Leaping onto the uppermost step, beneath the carved crystal archway of the grand entrance, he aimed an accusing finger at the statue of the empress upon her pedestal. "There she is," he hollered, "the architect of this entire insane enterprise."

Not far away, but separated from this moment and place by a phase or two of reality, a time-lost starship captain flinched at the word "enterprise" as he heard it translated into his own tongue. The name reminded him of dangers and responsibilities he was not being allowed to face. "Q," he began.

"Sssh," Q hushed him, watching 0 and his younger self watching Gorgan watching the Rzom. "Pay attention, Jean-Luc. You may find the modus operandi quite instructive. I certainly did."

"Let's show the galaxy that we mean what we say," the Rzom youth continued, "that we refuse to blindly worship the past. Down with that monument to folly. Down with the empress!"

Incited by their spokesman, the mob of students rushed the statue, climbing onto the pedestal and throwing their weight against the marble figure. Horrified by this attempt at vandalism, a few of the older citizens tried to intervene, placing themselves between the statue and the next wave of demonstrators, but they were quickly shoved aside by the overexcited students. Fists were raised and angry words exchanged, prompting the safeties to take action at last. "Attention," the senior safety announced, her voice artificially amplified by a mechanism planted against the base of her throat. "Step away from the statue at once. This gathering is declared a threat to public order and is hereby terminated. All citizens are directed to refrain from further debate and to exit the plaza in an orderly fashion."

The safety's instructions chastened a fraction of those assembled, who froze sheepishly in their tracks, then began to slink away; lawlessness did not come easily to people who had known decades of peace and stability. But the majority of the students, whose memories were shorter and whose law-abiding habits were less deeply ingrained, ignored the safety, continuing to clamber over the marble monument like Belzoidian fleas swarming over an unguarded piece of cake, while shouting and cheering uproariously. They appeared to be having the time of their lives, much to the delight of Gorgan. Tools that enjoyed their work always performed better than those who had to be grudgingly forced to their tasks. He nodded approvingly as a jubilant young Rzom started swinging back and forth from the outstretched arm of the sculpted empress.

The senior safety, on the other hand, scowled grimly at the sight. She had been afraid of this; the disturbance had already escalated too far, too fast. Choosing not to waste time with any further warnings, she sent a silent electronic signal to her fellow safeties, then aimed the ring on her left forefinger at the youth hanging from the statue's arm.

A beam of directed energy, fluorescently orange,

leaped from the ring, targeting the would-be vandal, who instantly disappeared from sight. The safety smiled in satisfaction, knowing that the reckless youth had been painlessly transferred to a holding facility at headquarters several city blocks away. Not for the first time, she wondered how safeties had ever managed before transference technology became so convenient; she could just imagine the incredible nuisance of having to physically subdue and transport each offender before placing them into a cell.

Around the plaza, each of the five safeties used their rings to thin out the crowd of students attacking the monument. As expected, the mere sight of their friends being deleted from the scene was enough to discourage several of the students, who backed away from the statue and each other, clearly unwilling to spend the night in a pacification cell, and probably not too eager to explain to their parents and tutors exactly how they ended up there. The senior safety permitted herself a sigh of relief; for a few seconds there, she had worried that she'd waited too long before attempting to dispel the agitated crowd. Now, though, the situation seemed to be coming under control.

But the student leader, not to mention Gorgan, would not surrender so easily. Urged on by his anonymous muse, Jenole entreated his followers to carry on their crusade in the face of the safeties's resistance. "Don't give up!" he cried out. "This is our moment, our chance to demonstrate once and for all that we will not be herded into submission, that we can take control of our destiny no matter who stands against us!"

His words had an impact on his peers, who kept storming the statue even as their fellow rebels disappeared left and right. Cracks formed in the marble surface of the monument, branching out from each other like twigs on a tree branch. An ominous scraping noise emerged from the base of the stature, where the empress's sculpted feet met the pedestal below. Beams of light picked off the demonstrators as they climbed out onto the arms and shoulders of the statue, but new bodies replaced those that vanished almost as quickly as their predecessors were transferred away. "That's right!" Jenole encouraged them from the top of the steps. "Don't let them break our spirits with their cowardly ploys. Show them that the future belongs to us!"

"Doesn't he ever run out of breath?" the senior safety muttered to herself. Turning away from the besieged monument, she directed both her ring and her attention at the students' ringleader, who presented quite an inviting target as he posed before the palace, his garish red cloak flapping in the wind. With any luck, deleting that loud-mouthed boy would suck the wildfire out of the rest of the protestors.

No, Gorgan thought, shaking his head slowly. He would not allow the furor he had created to be so readily extinguished. As the safety took aim at

Jenole, Gorgan summoned his power by clenching his fists and pantomiming a pounding motion with his hands, tapping one fist upon the other with a steady, deliberate rhythm. Without even realizing he was doing it, Jenole mimicked the gesture, pounding his own fists together in time with his unseen mentor just as the transference beam locked on to him.

Nothing happened.

To the safety's astonishment, Jenole remained where he stood, defying her attempt to relocate him. She blinked and tried again, with equally nonexistent results. The safety did not understand, and Jenole looked a bit bewildered as well; neither of them had ever known a safety's equipment to malfunction before. Only Gorgan, his upper hand silently hammering the fist below, greeted this new complication with aplomb. *The surprises are only beginning,* he promised.

The confused safety wagged her hand from the wrist up, hoping she could somehow shake her ring back into life. When that proved futile, she sent a private audio transmission to the two nearest safeties. A lighted visual display sewn into her right sleeve instantly informed her of their ranks and identity numbers. "One-one-two-eight, six-seven-four, target subject at top of steps immediately. Priority *Skr'zta.*"

Responding without hesitation, two uniformed figures, previously facing the endangered statue, swiveled at the waist and directed beams of cadmium light at Jenole. Either ray, the senior safety knew, would communicate his coordinates to the central processor, initiating the transference. The outspoken student gulped visibly as the twin beams intersected upon his chest right above his heart, but he continued to make that peculiar pounding gesture, for reasons neither he nor the safeties truly understood.

Whatever he was doing was obviously working. The other safeties exchanged baffled looks as Jenole persisted in striking a dramatic pose overlooking the plaza, despite the best efforts of three safeties—and advanced Tkon technology—to remove him. Now it was the senior safety's turn to swallow nervously, flinching involuntarily as one of the empress's marble arms broke away from her body, plummeting onto the tiled floor of the plaza to shatter into two pieces. With her pacification ring rendered unaccountably impotent, the safety felt like she had lost her own arm as well. "Get the safeties," Jenole instructed the other dissidents. "Their rings are useless now. Don't let them stop us!"

That those last two statements were mutually contradictory did not bother any of the students, who divided their efforts between toppling the now-mutilated statue and assailing the safeties, who suddenly found themselves outnumbered and unarmed. No safety had carried any physical weapons for years; why bother when any implement that might be needed could be summoned instantaneously by means of their rings? All at once, the senior safety found herself longing for an old-fashioned meson rifle—or even a big stick.

She tried to summon reinforcements, only to discover that the communicator at her throat had gone as dead as the silicon ring on her finger. Gritting her teeth, she tried to will the ring back into operation, but the accursed thing couldn't even produce a faint orange glow anymore. Its failure—impossible, inexplicable—left her with no hope of quelling the disturbance, let alone protecting herself. A tide of shrieking students, intoxicated with the heady bouquet of insurrection, flooded over her. She felt frenzied hands grabbing her, tugging at her ring, nearly breaking her finger in the process. The ring slipped free, scraping her knuckles red, and the crowd tossed her aside. She went stumbling across the floor of the plaza, falling onto her knees and barely throwing her hands out in time to stop her face from hitting the hard ceramic tiles.

A moment later, there was a ghastly wrenching noise, as the statue was torn from its pedestal and its heavy weight crashed to the ground, shaking the tiles beneath her palms and knees. A marble head bearing a marble crown rolled across the plaza until it came to a rest only a few arm's lengths away from the shaken safety. Its features, once beautiful and serene, were now chipped and gouged, looking up at the night sky with only the scarred vestiges of its former grace.

The empress had fallen.

"Yes!" Jenole crowed to the students below him, Gorgan perching behind him like a shadow. "No one in the empire can ignore us now!" His victorious compatriots hooted and howled in jubilation, letting the battered safeties creep away to safety. A blond-haired girl danced atop the empty pedestal while her friends in the crowd tossed fragments of the shattered statue among themselves, claiming pieces as souvenirs.

"That's right, celebrate!" Someone tossed Jenole the head of the empress, which he held aloft triumphantly, his golden eyes aglow, his cheeks flushed with excitement. "We've won. The night is ours." His gaze swept over the throng of ecstatic students, making certain he had their full attention. "But this is just the beginning." Gorgan's lips moved soundlessly and the words emerged from Jenole's throat, his voice alive with passion and commitment. "But this is just the beginning. There's an industrial transfer station only a few blocks from here, down by the River Hessari, where thousands of cauldrons of pure *tmirsh* are marked for delivery to the Great Expenditure. Raw material, torn from our planet and our people, never to return!"

The rioters booed and shouted profanities. Gorgan felt his power grow with the crowd's intensity. This was just like the old days, before 0's downfall. *This time it will be different,* he vowed. *No one can hinder us.*

"Those cauldrons belong to us," Jenole declared, "and I say they're not going anywhere. Now is the time for us to take back our destiny." He dropped the defaced marble head and let it roll awkwardly down the steps into the crowd, eliciting a full-throated hurrah from his peers. "Those cauldrons are waiting for us," he asserted, pointing past the plaza toward the riverfront. "Are you with me?"

The crowd's response was both overwhelming and inevitable. Any possible opposition had either fled in retreat or succumbed to the revolutionary fever. Unwilling or unable to defy the mob, the governor remained locked inside his mansion, while fresh safeties, summoned no doubt by observers within the palace, cordoned off the plaza, reluctant to engage the demonstrators until the mystery of their equipment's failure could be adequately explained.

But there was no time for answers. Running down the steps, taking them two at a time, Jenole set off a stampede of eager and unthinking young men and women streaming toward the far end of the plaza—and the line of turquoise figures who waited to halt their progress. Seen from above, as Gorgon levitated above the fray, the rampaging students resembled a surging sea, their knotted tresses bobbing like waves driven by a storm.

The newly arrived safeties never stood a chance. A deluge of amok Rzom youth crashed against them, meeting only inactive technology, and broke through their ranks, pouring into the city streets and shattering the quiet of the evening with their chants and cries and uninhibited laughter. The gates of the transfer station presented even less resistance than the cordon around the plaza. The night shift stepped back, frightened and uncomprehending as their sons and daughters tore through the unguarded facility, wreaking havoc on data files and delicate apparatus, shoving fragile exports off transporter platforms and stasis units alike, then converging on the preservation dome where materials allocated for the Great Endeavor were kept until needed.

The pillar of steam that rose from the River Hessari as countless units of molten *tmirsh* were dumped into its rushing amethyst currents could be seen from one end of the city to another. Some said, and they were correct, that the gigantic plume of heated vapor was even witnessed by imperial satellites in orbit around Rzom, who transmitted the image instantaneously to the empress herself.

Gorgan basked in the satisfaction of a job well done. He had planted the seed. Now it was up to his allies to nurture and cultivate the crop.

Until it was time for the harvest.

Chapter Nine

In the tenth year in the reign of the empress:

THE IMPERIAL FLEET WAITED just past the asteroid belt that divided the inner worlds of the Tkon Empire, including Tkon itself, from their rebellious siblings beyond the belt. At the prime-control of the scout ship *Bastu,* at the forward tip of the formation, Null Pilot Lapu Ordaln stayed attuned to his long-distance surveyors and wondered if he could ever possibly be ready for what was to come.

A battle such as was about to take place had not been fought since the Age of Xora, innumerable generations ago. Indeed, it was practically unheard-of to have this many vessels in the void at one time; safe and effective travel by transference had largely rendered nullcraft obsolete, except for exploration and warfare. The average citizen had not needed to ride a rocket from one planet to another since his grandfather's time, at least until recently, when the present crisis brought commerce and contact between the empire and the rebel worlds to a halt. "Hell-wings," he cursed aloud. Why couldn't Rzom and the other outer planets simply go along with the Great Endeavor like the rest of the empire? What in Makto's name had driven them to mount this insane rebellion, putting everyone at risk? Rend it all, he had friends on Rzom, even a cousin or two. Why, then, this senseless war?

To be fair, sages and opinionators still argued about who had truly started the war, the empire trying to quell uprisings on the outer worlds, or the rebels encroaching on imperial space to sabotage the Great Endeavor. *Never mind who began it,* he told himself, trying to ready his spirits for the confrontation ahead. *Our job now is to end it, one way or another.*

He glanced around the habitation bulb of *Bastu,* exchanging a glance with his subpilot, Nasua Ztrahs, strapped into her own control less than an arm's length away. Aside from them, no other living creature breathed within the bulb; all of the vital functions of the vessel, including attack and defense modes, were operated by the ship itself, with its organic pilots ready to override the thinking chips only in the event of some genuinely unforeseen circumstance. One pilot was practically superfluous; a subpilot to take over if the prime was disabled was an extra level of redundancy, dictated as much by tradition as by cautious calculation. Besides, Ordaln thought bitterly, if there wasn't some flesh and blood at stake, how could you call it a war?

There. Here they come. The ship's surveyors detected the approach of the enemy armada, alerting the null pilot at the speed of thought. Funny, it still felt wrong to think of Rzom as the enemy. Defensive systems came to life all around the bulb as the cerebral imager projected three-dimensional graphics of the oncoming ships directly into his mind. He heard Ztrahs suck in her breath and knew that she had received the same input. Testing the imager compulsively, as if every component of *Bastu* had not already been checked out by imperial shipwrights, he confirmed that he could switch back and forth at will between a subjective ship's eye view of the battle to an objective, omniscient overview of the entire conflict. He was relieved to note that, just as their informants had reported, the imperial ships outnumbered their rebel counterparts at least three to one. *We'll make short work of them,* he thought, *no matter how bloody a business it proves to be.*

"For Tkon and the empress," he said, loud enough for Ztrahs to hear. It was a null pilot's job to maintain proper morale, even for a crew of two.

"For Tkon and the empress," she answered back, her voice tense but controlled. It dawned on Ordaln that she probably had friends and relations on the other side, too.

Then the first of the enemy vessels was upon them. . . .

Almost, (*) thought hungrily. The clash it had been waiting for was only instants away. At the moment, it sensed more dread than anger among the participants, more apprehension than aggression, but that would change once the fighting started. Hate would come to the fore, and then (*) would feed.

And feed well.

Holding the enemy within their sights, monitoring each other's advance to the tiniest degree, neither side took notice of a flickering sphere of crimson energy spinning fiercely less than a light-year away, emitting a faint red radiance that failed to register on either imperial or rebel sensors. (*) also observed the disparity in strength between the two forces, and resolved to address that problem soon enough. It held no favorites in the coming contest, only a determination that both victory and defeat be forestalled for as long as possible. Only the war itself mattered; the fury and strife were their own reward.

The imperial fleet fanned out in three dimensions, assuming a pyramid formation with its point aimed straight at the heart of the rebel armada, which responded by angling outward and away from their center, forming a sideways funnel whose open mouth expanded as if to swallow the advancing pyramid. For a brief moment, as the forward end of the armada spread out like concentric ripples upon the surface of a pond, it looked like the larger, imperial fleet might pass through the opposing forces without even engaging the enemy, but the imperial pyramid flattened out abruptly as the warships that comprised its base raced to intersect the circumference of the gigantic, empty loop the invading armada had become. All along the periphery of both fleets, imperial and rebel ships rushed headlong at each other, unable to evade direct confrontation any longer.

Not even (*) could tell which side fired first. As swiftly and nigh simultaneously as if a switch had been activated, bursts of incandescent energy jumped from ship to ship to ship, linking hundreds of nullcraft in an intricate and ever-shifting lattice of red and purple beams of light that knitted the edges of both fleets to each other, locking them into a taut, violently twisting tapestry that only total defeat or victory could rip apart. Projectile weapons, powered by their own destructive energies, carried the battle deeper into the masses of the opposing forces, arcing through the void to hurl themselves at inhabited vessels several hundred times larger than the unmanned missiles that perished in sacrificial blazes against the hulls of their targets. The narrowing space between the contending fleets filled with fire and debris.

Despite heavy shielding on the part of both adversaries, the furious exchange of armaments claimed its first casualties within minutes. Unscratched, untested void fighters, subjected to dozens of assaults from above and below, succumbed to destruction and/or decompression. Transitory flashes of unfettered plasma strobed the battle lines, sparking anguish and desire for revenge among the surviving combatants. Abstract political differences suddenly became deadly personal as pilots on both sides dived and ducked amid the chaos, striking back with every tactic and weapon at their command. More ships fell before the inferno, leaving the remaining ships ever more intent on exacting retribution.

(*) savored the unleashed hate and fury of the volatile humanoids within their metallic conveyances. Its only fear was that the hostilities would terminate too soon, before it had drained every last drop of sustenance from the unsuspecting mortals. Avidly, it examined the ongoing encounter, subjecting the entire battle to its keen and far too experienced analysis. How best, it meditated, to prolong the conflict?

Ironically, the ships, large and small, that comprised both fleets were virtually identical in design, not surprising considering that not long ago they had indeed composed a single unified force, before time and trouble outpaced their common ancestry. Only carefully guarded meson signatures kept allied vessels from firing upon each other in confusion. (*) rotated thoughtfully, seeing all the possibilities.

* * *

For the first few minutes, Lapu Ordaln found himself at the still, silent center of the storm. The Rzom nullcraft had all darted away to the perimeter, leaving behind an empty hole at the core of their formation. He experienced a moment of private relief at this momentary respite, even though he knew he couldn't allow the rebels to evade him this easily. If fortune was with Tkon, his comrades behind him would halt the enemy's advance long enough for *Bastu* to reverse course and catch up with the fight.

"Let's go get them," he stated decisively, while psionically urging his ship to switch to pursuit mode. *Bastu* executed a flawless crescent turn that sent them speeding toward the action, which, as the imager showed him, had already begun. In his mind's eye, he saw the fighting flare up at the outskirts of the rebel armada, then work its way inward, zigzagging through the rapidly intermeshing fleets like spidery cracks fragmenting a sheet of ice. The meson tracking system functioned perfectly, tracing imperial ships in blue and rebel vessels in red. To his dismay, he watched as, one at a time, graphics both blue and red vanished neatly from the display.

We could be next, he realized, feeling a bitter resentment toward the Rzom lunatics who had brought them all to this sorry pass. He wanted to look away, but the cerebral imager made that impossible. The more he squeezed his eyelids shut, the more clearly he saw the deadly conflagration that was drawing him closer by the second, like a charged particle to a blazing atomic core. He braced his back against the gravity cushion and tugged on the straps of his harness to make certain they were secure. *Bastu* was coming within range of its weapons capacity, not to mention close enough to draw fire from the enemy. Time to kill or be killed. Thank Ozari that the ship actually did the targeting, sparing him and Ztrahs that awful responsibility.

Without warning, the red and blue outlines marking each nullcraft disappeared from the display. His eyes opened wide in surprise, but the image remained the same. Suddenly there was no way to distinguish imperial ships from the rebels, friend from foe. *Bastu*'s attack systems froze even as the ship plunged into the melee, the thinking chips paralyzed by this unexpected loss of crucial data.

"Lapu?" his subpilot asked, confusion evident in her tone. Obviously she was receiving the same inadequate display from the imager.

"Reinitialize the entire system," he replied. "Do whatever you can to get the accursed thing up and running again. Quickly." In the meantime, he realized with a start, he would have to take over control of the weapons from the ship. He was fighting this war for real.

But what good could he do? *Bastu* weaved effectively through the crowded null-space, avoiding collisions with the other warships, but Ordaln did not know what else could be done. He couldn't just fire blindly; given the relative size of the fleets, he was more likely to hit one of his own ships than a rebel. "Lapu—I mean, Pilot Ordaln!" Ztrahs reported within moments, visibly aghast. "It's not just us. It's everyone, us and the enemy both. Nobody's markers are working."

How was that possible? A solar flare? A transreal anomaly? Ordaln didn't even try to figure it out; he was a pilot, not a techner. Instead his mind instantly grasped the strategic implications of what had happened; all at once, the empire's numerical superiority had become a liability. Without the meson tags, the rebels had better odds of hitting their enemies than he did.

"They did it on purpose!" he blurted, blood pounding in his temples as the truth struck him with the force of orbital acceleration. What manner of crazed, reckless ploy was this? Fighting in the dark like this might get them all killed. Didn't so many lives, Tkon or Rzom, mean anything to them? "They're insane, all of them! Fanatics!"

But he wouldn't let them get away with it. . . .

Yes, (*) approved, basking in the renewed waves of enmity suffusing the sector. The warriors of the inner planets would not overcome those of the outer worlds so easily now. Their frustration fed their animosity, feeding (*), just as the desperation

189

of all concerned only heightened the intensity of their violent passions. This was more than mere nourishment now; it was an exquisite delicacy.

(*) spun silently in the depths of space, lapping up the hate that spilled like blood. Best of all, it had not yet approached the very peak of its feeding cycle. The more the organic specimens hated, the stronger (*) grew, and the stronger it became, the better it could fan the flames of the conflict, toying with the minds and matter below it to yield ever greater rewards.

As it did now.

Rzom trash. It was all their fault.

Another shudder shook the habitation bulb as *Bastu* came under attack again. Ordaln unleashed a volley of concentrated plasma bolts at the nearest vessel, not caring terribly whether it hailed from Tkon or Rzom or any of the other worlds that had been dragged into this stinking bloodbath. They had attacked him, that was enough, so he emptied his arsenal at them, then waited for the pulse cannons to recharge.

Tkon can still win, he realized, *even with everyone shooting randomly. We can triumph by attrition, when the last rebel craft has been reduced to null-dust.* He just had to stay alive until then, and the best way to do that was to fire at anything that came within range of his weapons. "Blast them all, and let Ozari take Their pick," he growled, his throat bubbling over with bile. He launched a brace of cobalt missiles at a suspicious-looking scout ship at sixty degrees, and was gratified to see it spiral away in flames. "Isn't that right, Nasua?"

The subpilot was dead, killed by a jagged piece of silicon crystal that had broken through the habitation bubble during the last missile strike. Ordaln wasn't worried. She wouldn't be dead much longer. Already both pilot and bulb were repairing themselves, the crystal shard retracting back into *Bastu*'s internal mechanisms, the pierced plasteel shell of the bulb knitting itself shut miraculously. Time almost seemed to be running in reverse as the gaping wound in Ztrahs's throat closed, leaving not even a scar behind. Ordaln watched, unsurprised, at the way the color came back into her expression. Her lifeless golden eyes blinked, then looked back at him. "They killed me again?" she asked, sounding more annoyed than distressed.

"Yes," he replied curtly. It was nothing new; they had each been killed a couple times already. But Ozari would not let them die, it seemed, as long as the fight continued. Their wounds healed magically, their ship kept repaired, their weapons perpetually replenished . . . what more proof did they need that the fates were on their side? This had become a holy war, and Ordaln was more than happy to wipe the rebel dirt from existence, no matter how many times he had to die. He'd had friends among the Rzom, sure, and family, too, but they were nothing to him now, not anymore. All that mattered was winning the war, which meant destroying the enemy once and for all.

He launched more missiles, one in every direction, confident that no matter how many he fired, there would always be more. He was glad that he had taken control of the weapons himself. It was more satisfying this way. "Die, rebels, die!" he chanted, and Ztrahs joined in, laughing maniacally. "Death to the Rzom!"

And the battle went on and on. . . .

Chapter Ten

In the fiftieth year of the reign of the empress:

FAR FROM THE STRESSES OF WORK OR WAR, a photon wave engineer named Kelica udHosn stretched out upon a leased solo lifter and went fishing for birds. Elsewhere in the empire, there was strife and nullfleets were clashing, but not here on Wsor, deep in the heart of the inner worlds, between sacred Tkon and the dying sun. Kelica's shallow float drifted several lengths below a billowing bank of swollen tangerine clouds. A thin line of polynitrated filament stretched upward from the reel in her left hand to somewhere deep within the cloud directly overhead. A minus-grav hook, baited with a piece of raw *ewone,* waited for any unwary avians who might be lured by the glistening magenta pulp.

To be completely up-front about it, Kelica didn't

care if she caught a plump galebird or not. This was the first vacation she'd had from the Great Endeavor in what felt like a radioactive half-life and it was enough simply to waft through the sky on the gentle wind currents, the clouds above her, the rolling umber hills of the Maelisteen countryside far beneath. Yes, this was exactly what she needed after seven months of balancing and rebalancing the light index ratios for the proposed solar transference. For Ozari's sake, the tired old sun wasn't going to flare out anytime this week. The Great Endeavor could do without her for a few days.

She rolled onto her side and took a sip of the spicy nectar in the juiceskin beside her. An elevated calciate ridge, about a hand's breadth high, ran along the perimeter of her oblong lifter, preventing her from tumbling off its padded surface carelessly, even though she kept her emergency floater belt on just in case. She gazed out at the breathtaking scenery available to her from her lofty vantage point; aside from another float on the horizon, she had the whole sky to herself. That was the great thing about Wsor: As one of the innermost planets, the war with the outer worlds had barely touched it so far. Peeking over the edge of the safety ridge, she saw Proutu Mountain rising to the southeast, its snowcapped peak reflected in the glassy surface of Lake Vallos. A few small pleasure rafts, looking like discarded wood shavings from this high up, nestled atop the lake, prompting her to wonder why anyone would still go fishing the old-fashioned way when they could go trolling through the clouds instead.

Lazy minutes passed without a single tug on her line, and Kelica began to feel just the tiniest bit bored. Closing her eyes and activating the implant at the base of her brain, she tapped into the psi-network, her mind scanning the local emanations for something interesting.

People of Wsor, turn away from your sin and arrogance. Pay heed to The One who stands in judgment above you all. The days of your folly are numbered. Great is The One who comes from beyond. . . .

What was this, some kind of crazy religious wavecast? Might be good for a giggle or two, she decided as she adjusted her sun-warmed limbs against the cushions and took another sip of the nectar. The float coasted south toward the mountain, blown along by a cooling breeze.

. . . unto you and yours shall the overweening pride of your ancestors be held to account, even unto the end of days. Repent of your wayward paths, for The One will brook no impiety nor disrespect. Yea, even if no more than one soul shall turn away from The One, then all shall be punished. Many will fall before His Wrath, and those that live through the first chastisement will surely long for the sweet release of death. . . . .

Okay, okay, Kelica thought. She got the message, which was exhausting its novelty value at amazing speed. Who would actually want to listen to this blather? She searched for something else on the adjacent psi-bands.

. . . and the signs of His Judgment shall be written among the elements. Fire and water shall be His Rod and His Scourge, just as the rocks below and sky above. . . .

Huh? How did she get this again? She tried another neural frequency.

. . . and there shall be neither peace nor mercy, neither pardon nor deliverance. . . .

For the first time, she began to feel slightly nervous. The demented rantings seemed to all over the psi-scape, supplanting even the imperial news and weather wavecasts. She even tried accessing some of the more popular erotic transmissions, but to no avail. The apocalyptic warnings were everywhere, and expressly where they didn't belong.

Fall upon your knees and pray for salvation, but it shall not be forthcoming. The time for redemption has passed. Now comes The One and His Anger is great. . . .

It must be a psychological propaganda offensive, she realized, but how had the Rzom insurrectionists succeeded in hijacking the entire psionic network? And did they really expect modern-minded Tkon to fall for all this pompous mumbo-jumbo?

A yank upon her hand reminded her of her fishing line, which she had completely forgotten. Automatically she began reeling the taut filament in, too preoccupied by the unsettling wavecast to even wonder what she had caught. She was only planning to let the bird go anyway. She liked snaring the pretty birds, but saw no point in letting them suffer afterward. That was just pointless cruelty.

A deafening boom came without warning, the shock wave rocking the small lifter and tossing her backward against the cushions. Her elbow collided with the juiceskin, squirting nectar onto her side. Grabbing the safety ridge with her free hand, she pulled herself up to a sitting position and looked with amazement to the south.

The top of Proutu Mountain wasn't there anymore. Instead of the white-frosted peak she had admired only minutes before, a tremendous explosion of smoke and ash as large as the mountain itself gushed from an open crater, spewing flame and red-hot magma. Rivers of glowing lava poured over the jagged rim of the crater, racing the swiftly melting snow down the side of the mountain—no, the volcano!—and flooding into the wide-open reservoir of the lake, where a gigantic wall of steam rose into the air, obscuring her view of the mountain itself. The once-placid surface of the lake churned and bubbled, turning into an enormous cauldron of boiling mud and water.

Proutu had erupted. But that was impossible; the mountain had been extinct for aeons. All the travel data said so. And there hadn't been any signs or indications. No preliminary tremors, no geothermal disturbances. No warning at all, except:

Behold His Justice, and tremble. Look upon the

retribution of The One and know that the harrowing has just begun. . . .

"Sacred Ozari," she whispered. This couldn't be happening, but it was. Her ears still ached from that first cataclysmic detonation. A noxious odor, like sulfur or *macrum*, teased her nostrils. Ignoring the sticky wetness of the nectar spilling onto the floor of the float, she retained the presence of mind to press down with her thumb upon the release switch of her fishing reel, slicing through the filament and setting the unseen avian free. Then she looked back down at the frothing lake beneath her. None of the tourist rafts had overturned yet, but dead fish were floating to surface by the hundreds, turning the murky waters into a grotesque, colossal bouillabaisse.

. . . nothing shall be spared, neither the beasts of the field, nor the swimmers in the deep. . . .

Fortunately, the initial shock wave had sent her gliding away from the volcano. Thank . . . someone . . . that she hadn't been any closer to the mountain when it blew. She started to activate the auto-recall on the lifter, intending to get back to the launch center as quickly as possible, when she remembered the other float she had glimpsed earlier. Could that poor individual possibly have survived?

Holding the float in place by mental control, she peered back into the roiling fog of smoke and steam. The acrid smell was getting stronger by the moment; she could feel it stinging at the back of her throat. "Hello!" she called out hoarsely. "Is there anybody there?" There was no point scanning for a psychic cry for assistance; that malevolent sermon, which sounded like pure gloating now, was still raving across every psi-band, swamping everything else. She could hear that harsh, unforgiving voice bellowing inside her skull, no matter how hard she tried to shut it out. She shut down her implant entirely, but somehow the voice still came through.

. . . from the lower regions shall His Vengeance come. As blazing as an inferno is the sting of His Whip. . . .

Cupping her palm over her nose and mouth in a fruitless attempt to keep out the increasingly corrosive fumes, she squinted with teary eyes into the opaque black smoke. *I can't wait any longer, she thought. I have to turn back.*

Then she heard it

"Help me!" a strident voice cried out from behind the curtain of fog. It was a man's voice, steeped in terror. "Somebody help me!"

Kelica hesitated, unwilling to steer her own float into that lightless, tenebrous murk, but unable to abandon the desperate stranger lost in the dark. "Help, help me, please!" he screamed again, coughing loudly afterward. He sounded like he was choking.

To her relief, the prow of the other lifter poked from the sooty depths of the spreading smoke, pulling the rest of the craft behind it. That surge of hope was quickly replaced by fear when she saw that the unlucky air-fisher was no longer safely inside his craft, but was instead dangling by his fingertips from the edge of the float. "Don't panic," she whispered to herself, remembering the multiple safety measures built into the floater belt around his waist. He couldn't fall to his death if he tried. It was scientifically impossible. Of course, that was what they had said about Proutu erupting, too.

As the stalks fall before the scythe, so shall the unrighteous fall before The One. Nemesis is He, the leveler of nations, the purifier of worlds. . . .

Both man and floater were blackened with ash. Sooty tears ran like rivulets down his cheeks, streaking his face. "Just let go," Kelica called out, worried about colliding with the other lifter. They probably wouldn't hit hard enough to do any damage, but she didn't feel like taking chances. "Activate the minus-grav switch, and I'll come by and pick you up."

He tried to reply, but all that escaped his throat was a raspy cough. He nodded, though, and closed his eyes, mentally willing the belt into readiness. His straining fingers let go of the float—and he fell like a stone.

What! She couldn't believe it. The belt should have held him aloft. Why hadn't it worked? Her mouth hung open, too shocked to even breathe, while she watched the shrinking figure drop toward the boiling lake. *It's still all right,* she remembered. *The emergency transfer will kick in any second now, the moment he hits trigger velocity, transporting him back to the center and canceling his downward momentum.* She waited anxiously for the falling man to disintegrate into quantum particles.

It never happened. She stared in horror as he plummeted into the lake, the splash of his impact lost amid the churning chaos of the reservoir. Kelica gasped, sucking in air at last, only to choke on the caustic smoke. Panic set in, spreading through her like a fever. She had to get out of here now! *Back,* she ordered the lifter, grateful that she didn't have to breathe the word aloud. The fumes were getting worse, making her sick.

. . . and the kingdom of the air shall crumble, and the waters of life made into slaying venom. . . .

"Shut up, shut up," she snapped, pressing her hands against her ears. This was a nightmare. It couldn't be real. "Stop it. I don't want to hear it."

. . . and the orchards will be as deserts, and the skies as lifeless as the void. . . .

Something rough and feathery smacked against her head, then rebounded onto the sticky floor of the float. It was an adult galebird, its eyes glassy and immobile, its beak locked open in silent protest. She didn't need to feel for its hearts to know it was dead. The fumes, she realized. The gases from the volcano were killing the birds.

. . . from the meager to the mighty, from the lowly to the lords of the spheres, none shall escape The One. . . .

More downy bodies struck the lifter. They were falling by the dozens now. She held up her hands to shield her head as the shallow float teetered beneath the force of the avian downpour. The stricken birds began to pile up all around her, some of them still alive, their crimson wings weakly flapping, and a new fear struck her: What if the weight of the birds overloaded the capacity of the float? This was only a solo lifter!

Frantically, she started bailing out the bottom of the float, throwing the dead and dying birds over the side as fast as she could manage, heedless of the new feathered bodies slamming into her head and shoulders, buffeting the tiny craft while she wheezed for breath amid the suffocating smoke. But despite her frenzied efforts, the front of the float tipped downward alarmingly, throwing her forward onto her hands and knees among the grisly carpet of dead birds, their tiny bones crunching beneath her weight.

. . . for the greatest of the great is but a mote of foulness in the sight of The One, as the most flawless of gems is but a rough and coarsened stone in the face of His Glory. . . .

She wanted to flee the lifter, jump free of the float, but fright kept her frozen in place. What if her belt didn't work, either? She tried to activate either the minus-grav or the transfer alert, thinking at the belt so hard that her brain hurt, but nothing happened. She remained tethered by gravity to the foundering lifter, even as it began to spiral irresistibly toward the scalding water below, picking up speed as it carried her inexorably toward annihilation.

. . . thus shall perish the heretics and apostates, the blasphemers and nonbelievers, for I am The One, the alpha and omega, your beginning and your end. . . .

The last thing she saw, before the terrifying acceleration rendered her mercifully unconscious, was something almost too incredible to believe, even in the middle of a waking nightmare. It was the bottom half of the mountain where, impossibly, insanely, the flowing lava had carved a single word into the granite side of the mountain, like an artist affixing his signature to his latest masterpiece.

It was the ancient Tkon symbol for the number one.

Chapter Eleven

"AH, I LOVE THE LUSTER OF LAVA atop lesser life-forms," O rhapsodized. "Between you and me, Q, The One can be a bit overbearing at times, not to mention utterly humorless, but you have to admit that He puts His All into His Work."

"I spied a lush morsel on a banquet so vast," he chanted in his customary singsong fashion,

"That I wanted my fill as 'twere my last,
Among this spread that was all I could wish,
Never before had I seen such a dish,
Oh, never before had I seen such a dish."

The length and breadth of the Tkon Empire was spread out between them like a colossal game board. At the moment, the planet Wsor occupied the spotlight of 0's attention, which passed through the spinning globe and projected onto an adjacent plane of reality a magnified view of the volcanic devastation currently demolishing the southern continent, much as a lesser entity might use a holographic monitor. Rivers of molten lava, rendered several quadrillion times larger than life, oozed across the intangible screen, casting a crimson glow upon 0's grinning features as he levitated above the game board, being careful to keep the soles of his buckled shoes off the solar system below. Superimposed upon the magma, like a ghostly double image, were the stern and unforgiving features of The One. "Didn't I tell you this only got better?" 0 asked.

"It's certainly dramatic enough, I suppose," Q answered. He hung upside down on the reverse side of the board, his knees wrapped around a stretch of sturdy quantum filaments while his head dangled only a light-year or so above (or below, depending on your orientation) the diverse worlds of the empire. To be honest, he was starting to get distinctly disgusted, but it struck him as impolite to say so. 0's confederates had been at work for some time, at least half a century by Tkon standards, and yet all their games, no matter how creatively conceived, seemed to arrive at the same conclusion: lots of death and devastation and screaming. Which had a certain crude shock appeal at first, granted, until it became unpleasant and monotonous. *Frankly,* he thought, *I'd appreciate a little comic relief at this point, maybe even a nice roman-tic interlude.* He avoided 0's gaze as he let his mind wander. *I wonder what Q is doing right now?*

"About time you thought of me," his sometime girlfriend and future wife replied indignantly, flashing onto the scene. She stood just out of reach, oriented along the same axis as Q, so that he found himself staring directly into her kneecaps. "I was starting to wonder if I was going to cross your mind anytime before the heat death of the universe."

Q somersaulted off his invisible trapeze, landing on his feet in front of Q. Arms crossed atop her chest, she fixed a pair of dubious eyes upon him. Her auburn tresses fell across her shoulders, less elegantly coifed than they would be aboard the *Enterprise-E* six hundred millennia from now, but the arch of her eyebrow was no less haughty.

Despite her forbidding expression and body lan-guage, Q was glad to see her. Where was the fun of embarking on a bold new adventure if there was no one around to show off for? 0 and his pals didn't count; they were part of the experiment, and too experienced in this kind of thing to be either impressed or shocked by Q's role in the proceed-ings. *I need an audience,* he decided, and he couldn't think of anyone better than Q.

"Well?" she demanded, her face as frozen as absolute zero.

Apologies were only embarrassing, he decided. Better to simply brazen this one out. "Q! Great to see you! Come to join the fun?"

"Hardly," she said scornfully, shaking her head.

"Say, who have we here?" 0 called out. In a blink, he joined them on the opposite side of the game board. The projected scenes of volcanic havoc disappeared from view. "Aren't you going to introduce me to your fine female friend, Q?"

"Oh, right," Q muttered, slightly discomfited by the reality of having to deal with both 0 and Q at the same time. They each came from completely different slices of his existence, engaged separate aspects of his personality. It was like trying to be two different people at once. "0, this is Q. Q, this is 0. He's not from around here."

"So I hear," she said icily, regarding the stranger with all the warmth and affection she might lavish on a Markoffian sea lizard before turning her back on him. "I need to talk to you, Q . . . alone."

0's face darkened ominously at the female Q's not terribly subtle snub, reminding Q a little too much of how he had looked right before he flash-freezed the Coulalakritous. Then 0 saw Q watching him, and his expression lightened, assuming a more amiable mien. "Of course," he agreed readily. "Far be it from me to intrude upon such a charming young couple. The last thing you two need is a crusty old chaperon such as myself. If you'll excuse me, m'dear, I'll be stepping out for a while." Tipping his head at the female, he opened a doorway into another continuum, then stepped halfway through. "Don't be all day, Q," he warned, lingering for a moment between dimensions. He cast a glance at the expanse of the Tkon Empire as it waited beneath their feet. "The best is still to come. Mark my words, you haven't seen anything yet."

The doorway closed behind him, disappearing along with 0. *I wonder what he has in mind,* Q thought, intrigued by his new friend's cryptic promises. More apocalyptic destruction, or something more interesting? He looked forward to finding out.

His significant other didn't seem curious at all. "Finally," she huffed. "I thought he'd never leave." She surveyed the game board skeptically, as if she half expected to find 0's muddy footprints all over the unsuspecting empire. "All right, Q, what's this all about?"

"Er, what do you think it's all about?" Not the most brilliant retort he had ever come up with, but perhaps it might buy him enough time to think of something more clever. How best to present the situation to her anyway, and precisely what sort of reaction did he hope to elicit? It was hard to say, especially when he had mixed feelings himself about what The One and his associates were doing to the Tkon.

"Don't get coy with me, Q," she warned. "The Q told me all about the disreputable gypsy vagabonds you've been hanging around with. Really, Q, I thought you had better taste than to fraternize with entities so . . . parvenu."

Ordinarily, he found her impeccable snobbishness delightfully high-handed, but not when it was turned against him. Who was she to pick out his friends for him, as if he lacked the judgment and maturity to choose his own company? It was insulting, really. "You don't know anything about them," he said defensively, "and neither do the Q. I'll have you know that 0 and the others bring a fresh new perspective to this part of the multiverse. I may not agree with everything they're about, but I would certainly never dismiss their ideas out of hand simply because they're not part of our own boring little clique. *I* have an open mind, unlike other certain other Qs I might name."

A pair of ivory opera glasses appeared in her hand, and she glanced down at the sprawling interstellar empire beneath them. As she inspected the goings-on there, she shared what she saw with Q. A montage of moving images unfurled before his eyes, all taken from the daily lives of the present generation of Tkon: battle-weary soldiers crawling through the trenches of some Q-forsaken tropical swamp, a hungry child wandering lost amid the rubble of an obliterated city, angry rioters shouting through a hastily erected force field at uniformed troops, priceless manuscripts and ancient tapestries hurled onto a bonfire by chanting zealots, a spy on trial for her life before a military tribunal, even an assassination attempt on the life of the empress.

"Is this what you call a fresh perspective, a bold new idea: making life miserable for a tribe of insignificant bipeds?" She snapped the lorgnette shut with a flick of her wrist, terminating the picture show. "It's as tedious as it is tragic. Why don't you just peel the scales off an Aldebaran serpent while you're at it? Or pull the membrane off an amoeba?"

"At least they're doing something," Q pointed out, not entirely sure how he ended up defending 0's mysterious agenda, but too irritated to care. "They take an interest in matters outside the rarefied atmosphere of your precious Continuum. True, this sort of hands-on approach can get a bit messy, but it's no worse than the ghastly foolishness that developing species always inflict on themselves anyway. Remember those divers throwing themselves into the jaws of monsters back on Tagus? They turned themselves into fish food voluntarily, just for the sake of a primitive ritual, so what's wrong with sacrificing a few million more to a good end? Their tiny lives are measured in micronano-aeons, after all."

"Is that so?" she answered. "Who are you trying to convince, me or yourself?"

Good question, he thought, although he wasn't about to admit it. "I don't need to convince you of anything. I'm perfectly capable of making my own decisions."

"Particularly when they're the wrong ones. . . . Oh, don't make that face at me. This is more important than your wounded male ego." Her expression softened a tad as she tried one more time to get through to him. "Listen to me, Q. We've known each other ever since we've been able to manipulate matter and recite the pledge of omniscience at the same time. We learned how to parse the lesser atomic force together. Trust me when I say that I'm only looking out for your best interests here. Forget about this 0 character and his low-life confederates. I promise I won't think any less of you if you come away with me now."

"And then what?" Q asked, less heatedly than before. Although touched by her concern, he wasn't ready to surrender just because she had started firing roses instead of ammo. "Am I supposed to just creep back to the Continuum with my hypothetical tail between my legs, to sit back meekly with folded hands while the great big universe goes by?" He struggled to make her understand. "Don't you see, I can't give up now. This is the first time I've ever taken a risk, done something with my immortality. I'm not a kid anymore. It's high time I hold to my guns, stand by my mark, draw a line in the ether, and all that decisive stuff. Right or wrong, I have to see this through to the end, no matter what. It's the only way I'll ever find out who I really am."

"But this isn't about you," she protested. "It's about 0 and his crazy games. He's just using you."

"Maybe so," Q agreed, "but he can't take advantage of me without my cooperation. That's my choice to make, so, you see, it really does come back to me."

She sighed and shook her head sadly. "If you don't know who you truly are, then you're the only intelligence in the Continuum who doesn't. You're stubborn and unpredictable, Q. A volatile catalyst in the never-ending chemical reaction that is creation, the spice in the primordial soup. You have all the verve and vitality of the cosmos and not one iota of common sense." She dropped her opera glasses into the glowing red sun at the center of the Tkon Empire and watched as they bubbled and melted away. "And I suppose that's why I'm never going to be able to convince you to do the sane and rational thing and listen to me for once."

"No," Q confirmed, "although you wouldn't be you if you didn't keep trying now and then." Beyond that, he wasn't sure how to respond to her spontaneous description of him. *I kind of like that bit about the spice,* he thought, more than a little flattered, *although I could have done without the commentary on my common sense, or lack thereof.* "Thanks a lot, I guess."

"Good-bye, Q," she said before transporting away. "Don't say I didn't warn you."

Why should I, he reflected, *when I know you'll always be there to remind me?*

Young Q gazed ruefully at the empty space that his highly significant other had occupied only milliseconds before, seemingly saddened by her departure. Theirs had been a bittersweet parting, at best. "Just wait," he promised the starry blackness beside him. "We'll look back at this and laugh some-day."

"Not to worry, lad," a bombastic voice assured him. 0 materialized in the space the female had vacated. He looked much happier now that the distaff Q was gone. "She'll come around eventually, see if she doesn't." He threw back his head and chuckled heartily. "Women! They're the same in every reality. Why, the stories I could tell you!" He gave Q a solid punch in the shoulder that sent him stumbling sideways. "But I don't need to teach a strapping young rooster like you about the fairer sex, do I? I imagine you've got a girl in every solar system or my name isn't 0!"

Several meters away, unseen and unheard by either participant in this one-sided discussion, Jean-Luc Picard groaned aloud. "I can't believe you actually fell for all this phony masculine cama-raderie," he told the Q standing beside him.

"Cut me some slack, *mon capitaine*," he said. "I was barely seven billion years old. What did I know about the ways of extra-dimensional executioners?"

"Executioner?"

"Just watch the show, Jean-Luc," Q advised sourly, "before I regret bringing you here in the first place."

Chapter Twelve

LEM FAAL FELT LIKE AN ULLAFISH fighting its way upstream. As he staggered down the seemingly endless corridors of the *Enterprise* in search of Engineering, pockets of uniformed crew members kept streaming past him on the way to sickbay, getting in his way. *Idiots,* he cursed. Didn't they realize he had more important things to do than let them pass by in their pointless attempts to preserve their own insignificant existences? Immortality was within his grasp, but these blinkered Starfleet buffoons were doing their best to obstruct him, especially that pigheaded fool Commander Riker.

Wheezing painfully, he slowed long enough to brace himself against a sturdy duranium wall. He could feel the constant hum of the Calamarain vibrate through the metal. His lungs felt like they were wrapped in barbed wire, and the corridor seemed to swim before his bloodshot eyes. He reached for his hypospray, then remembered that he had emptied its contents into Counselor Troi, feeling a flicker of guilt at having treated a fellow Betazoid so badly. *I had no choice,* he rebuked his conscience. *They were going to put me in stasis, shut down my brain just when I need it most. There was nothing else I could do. I* had *to get away.*

The barrier was all that mattered, and the voice in his mind beckoning to him from beyond the great wall. That voice had promised him life, plus knowledge and power beyond mortal understanding. *Come soon,* the voice whispered even now. *Soon, sooner, soonest. Soon, come soon. Closer to me, closer to you, closer . . .*

All he had to do was create the wormhole, break through the barrier to the other side. Then he would be saved, would be spared from his own terrifying mortality. He would never stop, never cease to be, as Shozana had when she had disappeared before his very eyes.

Your eyes are my eyes are yours. View you, view I . . .

He closed his eyes, seeking relief in the darkness for just a second. Odd . . . he could barely remember his wife's face now; all he could see was the column of energized atoms she had become when the transporter malfunctioned. *I shall become pure energy, too,* he thought, *but in a different, more transcendent way.*

215

"Sir, are you all right? Can I help you?"

Coming closer, closer coming, closer . . .

He opened his eyes and saw the concerned face of a minor Starfleet officer, a Benzite from the looks of him. Puffs of essential gases escaped from the respiratory device positioned beneath his nostrils. Faal noted a large orange bruise upon his bluish green forehead. "What?" the scientist asked. He could barely hear the officer's words over the voice calling out to him, growing stronger and louder the nearer they came to the barrier.

The wall divides us, the wall is nigh . . . deny the wall, and hopes are high . . . heigh, heigh, heigh!

The more clearly he heard the voice, the more enigmatic its words became. It spoke in riddles, as sacred oracles have always done, but Faal had deciphered its message from the beginning. Eternal life and enlightenment waited beyond the galactic barrier.

The wall is nigh, the wall deny . . . heigh, high hope, heigh.

"You don't look well, sir," the Benzite said. "I'm on my way to sickbay." He held a sleeve that was stained with whatever Benzites used for blood. Tiny droplets peeled off the torn fabric and floated in the weightless corridor. "Can I help you there?"

"No," Faal wheezed. He shook his head, then regretted it; the motion caused the floor to spin beneath his feet even faster than before. It took all his concentration to make his tongue move the way it had to, say the words the Benzite needed to hear. "The wall is . . . I mean, I have to get to engineering. Mr. La Forge needs me," he lied.

Closer to the wall, closer to the All . . .

The Benzite looked dubious. He assessed Faal's heaving chest and trembling limbs. "Are you sure, sir? No offense, but I don't think you're in any shape to assist anyone."

Why won't he leave me alone? Faal thought desperately. Every moment he was kept away from his goal was a torture. *Closing on the wall, or is the wall closing on you, closing the door . . . ?* He wanted to hurl the overly solicitous officer away, consign him to oblivion, but instead he had to waste precious moments allaying the concerns of this nonentity. *Close, closing, closer* . . . "I'm all right," Faal assured him, forcing himself to smile reassuringly. "I'm not injured, just a little closer . . . that is, just a little ill. It must be the weightlessness."

"Oh, right." The Benzite nodded his head. "I wouldn't know. Benzites don't get nauseous."

"You're very fortunate, then," Faal gasped. *Come closer to me closer to you, soon, sooner, soonest.* "But I'll be close . . . fine . . . if I can just make it to a turbolift."

"We're at red alert, sir," the Benzite pointed out helpfully. "The turbolifts are only for emergency use."

"This *is* an emergency, you dolt!" He couldn't hide his impatience any longer. The ship was approaching the wormhole. He had to get to engineering, launch the torpedo containing the magneton generator, force La Forge to initiate the subspace matrix, create the artificial wormhole, liberate the voice. . . . There was so much to do in so little time, and this blue-skinned, gas-sniffing cretin would simply not let him be. "The voice is calling me. I have to go!"

Soon, sooner. Come to the wall, come soon . . .

Lurching forward, away from the duranium bulkhead, he grabbed the Benzite's wounded arm and shoved it roughly. The crewman's blood felt slick and greasy against his palm, but the Benzite emitted an inarticulate croak and crouched over in pain, gasping so hard that the fumes wafting from his respirator dissipated before reaching his nostrils. *Serves you right,* Faal thought vindictively.

More Starfleet personnel came around the corner ahead, a man and two women, in scorched gray uniforms. Faal breathed a sigh of relief that they had not arrived in time to see him accost the Benzite. "He's hurt badly," he blurted hastily, pointing back at the breathless Benzite. "Hurry. Please help him." He pushed his way past them, urging them onward, then hurried around the corner until they were out of sight. *Hurry, hurry, hurry . . . come soon come.* If fortune was with him, the Benzite wouldn't be able to speak clearly for a few more moments, giving him time to get away.

The time is nigh, the wall is high, defy the nigh high wall . . . try!

The barbed wire tore at his lungs with every breath and his heart was pounding alarmingly, but he refused to let his debilitated physical state slow him down. He was more than this decaying shell of crude flesh and bone. His mind could overrule the limitations of his treacherous body and soon would be able to do far more than that. *I'm coming,* his mind called to the voice beyond the way, the voice that had summoned him all the way from Betazed, enticed him away from his children and his deathbed. *Do not forsake me. I will bring down the wall. I will, I swear it.*

Closer to the wall, closer . . . closer . . .

He was tempted to shed the cumbersome gravity boots and simply soar down the hall, but more realistically, he feared losing control of his momentum, at worst ending up becalmed in the air out of reach of any convenient wall or ceiling. What did he know about maneuvering in zero-G? He was a scientist, not an athlete. No, it was safer just to walk on his own two feet, no matter how weary they were.

Feel you closer, closer you feel me closer . . .

A turbolift entrance beckoned to him from the end of the corridor. Shallow breaths whistling from his diseased lungs, he propelled himself down the last few meters until his hands smacked against the sliding metal doors—which refused to open. "Let me in!" he demanded, pounding on the doors with his fists. The blood of the Benzite left a sticky stain on the painted surface of the door.

A dismayingly calm voice, which he had come to know as the ship's computer's, responded promptly, "The turbolifts are not currently available to unauthorized personnel. Civilian passengers should report to either sickbay or their quarters."

He let out a moan of despair. It was just as the Benzite had foretold. Intellectually, he understood the reasoning: Starfleet didn't want people to become trapped in the turbolifts while the ship was under attack. But what did that matter when his very future was at stake? It was all the Calamarain's fault, he realized. *You should have warned me about them,* he accused the voice.

Smoke, it answered obscurely. *Nothing but smoke to choke and choke.*

Faal didn't understand. If not for the lack of gravity, he would have slumped to the floor. Instead he let his magnetic boots anchor him to the floor as his exhausted frame swayed from left to right. He listened to the thunder of the Calamarain booming against the ship, and cursed the day he ever heard the name *Enterprise.* He would sooner have stayed on Betazed, helpless and dying, than endure the infinite frustration of coming so close to salvation, only to be stopped in his tracks by a balky turbolift.

No smoke in the wall, none at all, none at all . . .

Then, as the voice foretold, the thunder fell silent. The metal doors beneath his palm ceased to vibrate in unison with the alien hum. *The Calamarain,* he realized instantly, *they're gone.* Which meant, he deduced almost as quickly, that the *Enterprise* must have just entered the barrier.

Into the wall, closer to the All . . .

A sense of awe, mixed with dread and anticipation, passed through him only a heartbeat before his entire body was jolted by an intense psychic shock that raced through his nervous system, electrifying him. His spine and limbs stiffened, his arms stretched out at his sides. Tiny traceries of white energy linked his splayed fingers like webbing. His muscles jerked spasmodically and his eyes glowed with silver fire. Although no one was around to see it, the scientist flickered in and out of reality, transforming into a photonegative version of himself and back again. The pain in his lungs, the aching exhaustion in his joints vanished at once, driven out of his awareness by the supernatural vitality coursing through his body. *It's the power of the barrier,* he realized, *filling me, transforming me.*

But more than just mindless energy was pouring into his brain, expanding his mind. He sensed a personality as well, or at least a fragment of one, the same personality that had called to him for so long, promised him so much. *Yes . . . feel you closer, so close so closer . . . yes.* The voice brushed his soul, like the delicate touch of a spider's leg, and

Greg Cox

another identity, older and vastly more powerful, met and melded with his own. For one brief millisecond, Faal's self reeled with fear, protective of his unique individuality, but then it was submerged beneath the alien memories and sensations that seemed inextricable from the power he now possessed, the voice that was possessing him. *You are I are you, view I, view you . . .*

The face of that strange, meddling entity, Q, appeared in his memory, now bringing with it a sense of anger, of long-simmering hatred, that he had not previously known. *Q, cursed Q, treacherous Q . . . what will we do, to Q and Q and Q . . . ?*

Frantic to hang on to some trace of what he was, Faal tried again to visualize his wife's face, but instead all he could see was that other Q, the female one with the astounding child, the child of the Q. The power of the barrier, and the voice beyond, flooded his synapses, setting off a cascade of memories that the power seemed to sort through at will, picking and choosing according to its own unfathomable agenda. *Yes, yes,* he thought, no longer capable of distinguishing his own desires from those of the voice, *the child is the future, the child is our future, in the future the child. . . .*

Unable to cope any further with the forces at work within, Faal blacked out, his sagging limbs floating limply above the floor while dreams of apotheosis brought themselves to life.

Close, so close. . . .

* * *

222

Where is he? Milo wondered. He was lost and couldn't find his father anywhere. He had tried to take a turbolift, hoping to catch up with his dad at Engineering, only to discover that they had all shut down during the emergency. In theory, that meant his father was stuck on this level, too, but this ship was so huge, with so many corridors and intersections to choose from. To be honest, Milo wasn't sure he could find his way back to sickbay if he tried. *Dad!* he called out with his mind. *Come back!*

He couldn't sense his father's thoughts anywhere, no matter how hard he concentrated. It was like his father had cut himself off completely from the rest of the world, or at least from his son. *I don't even know who he is anymore,* Milo thought. The father he knew, the one he remembered from before, never would have attacked the counselor like that.

Milo stomped down another hallway, feeling clumsy in his oversized magnetic boots. Maybe he *should* try to find sickbay; Dr. Crusher and Counselor Troi had been very insistent about using the cortical stimulator on him before the ship entered the galactic barrier. Thank the Sacred Chalice that Kinya was safe at least, even if he and Father were in danger. His throat tightening, he wondered who would take care of her if . . . something happened . . . to his father and him. *Aunt Mwarana would take care of her, I guess.*

A crew member, rushing down the corridor toward him, spotted Milo and slowed to a stop.

"Hello?" she said. "What are you doing wandering around at a time like this?"

"Um, I'm looking for my father," he mumbled. How could he begin to explain how crazy his father had become, what he had done to poor Counselor Troi? "I think he was going to Engineering, but I'm not sure if he got there."

The woman hesitated, chewing on her bottom lip, torn between her own urgent errand and the plight of the boy. He could sense her indecision and concern. She reached a decision quickly, though, just like a Starfleet officer. "My name is Sonya Gomez, and I was on my way back to Engineering from sickbay anyway." Milo noticed a foam cast around her left wrist and sensed some residual soreness from the injury. "Why don't you come along with me and we'll see if your father is there? If not, I'm sure we can spare someone to see you back to your quarters."

"Okay," Milo said. He sure couldn't think of a better plan. Gomez held out her hand, and Milo accepted it gratefully. She began to lead them down the corridor in the same direction he had just come when she suddenly stopped and cocked her head. A quizzical expression came over her face. Milo felt a surge of optimism within her heart.

"Hey, listen to that," she said. "The thunder's stopped."

She's right, Milo thought. He would have said so, except for the blazing fire that ignited inside his skull. His small frame convulsed unexpectedly, like he was being electrocuted. He heard Sonya Gomez shouting in alarm from somewhere very far away. She shook his shoulders, but he couldn't feel it, not like he could feel the fire as it poured from his brain into the rest of his body, causing his entire body to tingle and twitch.

His eyes rolled upward and he lost consciousness, but instead of falling into blackness, all he found waiting for him was a brilliant purple light.

Chapter Thirteen

GLEVI UT SOV, DOWAGER EMPRESS OF TKON, awoke early one morning during the dawning of the Age of Makto, in the eightieth year of her reign, troubled by the shadows of unremembered dreams. She no longer slept as well as she once had. A symptom of her advanced age, she wondered, or of the increasing precariousness of the times? Her reign had been a turbulent one, marked by civil war and catastrophe, although she remained steadfast in her conviction that the Great Endeavor was worth any sacrifice she and the empire had endured. *Only my conscience does not plague me,* she thought.

Unlike her decrepit body, her private chambers had changed little over the decades. Skilled artisans had successfully concealed any evidence of the damage inflicted by the earthquake of seven years ago, or by the bomb that had failed to assassinate her only a few months before. She permitted herself a defiant smile; sometimes her stubborn ability to survive impressed even her. *They'll not get rid of me that easily,* she vowed, not for the first time.

She kneaded her weary eyes with skeletal knuckles, wishing she could clear her mind as readily. What had that dream been about anyway? The memory lurked at the back of her awareness, just beyond her reach, but the feeling remained, a sense of alarm mixed with inspiration, as if she had finally isolated the root cause of all that disturbed her suffering empire. There *was* a root cause, of that much she felt certain; over the last several decades, as she had assiduously studied reports from all over the empire, she had grown convinced that there was a reason for the numerous, often seemingly unrelated adversities that had rocked the foundations of their society for all these many years, a reason that sometimes seemed to lurk just beyond the awareness of her consciousness. Perhaps this latest dream held the key to an answer she already knew deep within her soul.

She knew better than to chase the memory, however. Dreams were like fish: The harder you tried to hold on to them, the more slippery they seemed to be. If it was important, it would come back to her in time. After all, she wasn't planning to die right away, at least not today.

Doing her best to ignore the creaking noises that, perversely, her hearing remained keen enough to detect, she carefully lowered her feet into the well-worn slippers on the floor. Despite the incessant appeals of her attendants, she still refused to let anyone help her aged bones rise. As long as she could stand, however shakily, on her own two feet, so, she was convinced, would the empire. It was a silly superstition, but she held to it nonetheless.

The chambers lighted slowly, as was her preference these days. She took a moment to steady herself, then reached out and grasped the sturdy walking stick propped against the wall by her couch. A polished quartz rendition of the Endless Flame emblem topped the stick. Her shadow, now much thinner than she might like, waited patiently for her to begin their daily trek to her venerable desk. With a sigh, she obliged the shadow by putting one foot before the other. The soles of her slippers squeaked as she shuffled across the floor.

As ever, the outer rooms felt too cold for comfort, so she gave the chamber a mental command to increase the temperature by at least ten grades. That she could effect such a change merely by thinking it still amazed her; out of habit, she often spoke aloud to her palace, much to the whispered amusement of the younger members of her court.

A finger unconsciously stroked the base of her skull where, beneath her snow-white hair and delicate skin, her personal psi-transmitter had been implanted. All her physicians and technologists swore to her that she couldn't possibly feel anything from the implant. You won't even know it's there, all the brilliant young geniuses insisted; everybody has one these days. No doubt they knew what they were talking about, but she was positive she felt an itching at the back of neck sometimes, not to mention a faint buzzing in her ears. *Maybe I'm just imagining it,* she thought, *just like I imagined whatever I dreamed last night.*

Placing her stick against the side of the desk, she sat down in her chair, grateful for the extra heat that was already flooding the chamber. She supposed she could just keep the heat going continuously, so that the chambers would always be warm right from the start, but that struck her as extravagantly wasteful, especially during wartime. Given all the sacrifices she had demanded of her people over the years, all the resources poured into the Great Endeavor despite every crisis that had threatened to derail it, the least she could do was cope with a bit of chill upon waking, especially when she suspected that a good part of the cold was simply her aging metabolism taking its time to come up to speed each morn.

She directed a thought at the freshly restored wall across from her and the city presented itself to her once more, lifting her spirits. Ozari-thul still rose proudly beneath the ruddy glow of dawn. True, many towers were under repair while wary imperial fliers patrolled the skies above them, but the heart of Tkon still beat as soundly as her own, the people going about their business even in the face of terrorism and sabotage. The scarlet sun confessed its mortality every day, yet the time was swiftly approaching when the slow death of that ancient orb would no longer endanger the worlds and people now within its radiance. *I cannot betray their confidence in me,* she thought. *The Great Endeavor must be completed.*

A twinge of hunger interrupted her musings and, in response, her breakfast appeared atop the desk. The biscuits and jam were tempting, and to blazes with what her doctors said about the honey, but she pushed the tray aside for the moment. Something, perhaps the lingering influence of that elusive dream, compelled her to check on her empire first.

Gazing down upon the tinted crystal disk, newly replaced after the bombing, she retrieved the latest bulletins. As usual, it made for depressing reading. New fighting along the intermediate orbits. Two more ships lost and a nebular mining station fallen to the rebels. Demonstrations and work stoppages throughout the inner worlds, even rumors that the governor of Wsor was secretly trying to negotiate a separate peace with Rzom in exchange for neutrality in the war. A devastating jungle fire on the fourth moon. Mass suicides among the commerce artists. A blight on this season's crop of *tamazi,* plus an outbreak of melting fever in the provinces of Closono-thul. Intelligence reports on a new millennial cult calling for the preordained destruction of Tkon. Flooding along the canals on Dupuc. A massacre on the second moon of a planet she had never heard of before.

On and on it went. Disasters. Combat. Epidemics. Accidents. Atrocities. Raids. Carnage. Fatalities. Revolts. Armed incursions . . . bad news from every corner of the empire, loyal or otherwise. The only consolation was that the rebels seemed to be hurting just as much, which was cold comfort indeed; despite close to a generation of internecine conflict, she still thought of the outer planets as under her protection, even if she had to fight to save them from themselves. The war itself had turned into one long, bloody stalemate in which neither side could gain any lasting advantage over the other. Was that the fault of her generals, she wondered, or were there other factors at work?

A piece of her dream flashed across her consciousness, almost too quickly to identify. Something about a captive beast . . . and spears? She reached for it, but it slipped away as quickly as it came. *Patience,* she counseled herself. *Let it come at its own speed.* She had learned to trust her dreams over the course of her lifetime, much as her visionary ancestors must have. *Don't force it. Wait.*

The image felt oddly familiar, though, as if she had dreamed it before, perhaps many times before, without ever remembering it. *Until now,* she thought, *to some degree.*

Turning her attention away from ephemeral fragments of the night before, she lifted a biscuit, generously drenched in honey, to her lips, then put it down again. "Too late," she sighed. The endless litany of dire news reports had killed her appetite.

She stared again into the disk, looking for some sign of a pattern, of a common thread linking all the disparate hardships tormenting her people. There was a link, she suddenly felt convinced. Her dream had told her so, even if she couldn't yet recall how it went. Perhaps the answer lay, she thought, in those *other* reports, the ones that didn't appear to make sense at all, that hinted in fact at the supernatural.

These strange, unexplainable incidents had been part of the bulletins for years, although often hidden in the margins or between the lines. Usually described as "apocryphal" or "unconfirmed," they had remained eerily consistent over the decades: accounts of dead soldiers rising up to fight again, of carefully maintained technology failing without cause, of storms and hurricanes birthed without warning out of clear skies and tranquil seas, of all manner of impossible occurrences taking place despite every precept of logic and science, just like that rain of *vovelles* that had fallen upon the city so many years ago, when she was barely more than a child. *I haven't thought of that for ages, but I suppose that's when it all started to go wrong.* A vision of swollen, overripe spheres of fruit pelting themselves against her windowpane, making wet, smacking noises while their juices ran like rivulets of blood down the transparent glass, surfaced from the dusty recesses of her memory. *It's almost as if some higher power were playing with us, testing us. . . .*

At once, her dream came back to her, more vivid than before. She saw a great horned animal at bay, its hooves pawing the ground, its curved ivory horns stabbing the air above its massive head. Its fur was dark and matted, except for a white patch upon its brow in the shape of a flame. Three masked figures, and two more farther back in the shadows, had the beast cornered, prodding it with long sharp sticks that drew blood wherever they pierced the animal's shaggy hide, but never enough to inflict serious injury on the beast. The wounds were like pinpricks, intended not to kill but only to torture and enrage. Maddened, the poor creature frothed at the mouth and blew steam from its snout, roaring its helpless fury even as the bloody spears came at it again and again.

Then, finally, when the beast could offer no further resistance, the masked tormentors laid down their spears and stepped aside, making way for the fourth figure to advance toward the vanquished animal, a shining silver blade resting in his grip. This fourth figure, to whom the others seemed to defer, wore no mask, but she could not discern his features no matter how hard she tried. All she could see was the light reflecting off the burnished sheen of the blade as he raised it high above the beast's drooping head. The fifth figure came forward finally, reaching out as if to stop the bearer of the sword, but he had waited too long. There was no more time, and the blade came sharply down—

The empress came back to her chambers with a

start, one hand jerking forward and knocking the breakfast tray over the edge of the desk. Crystalline plates and teacup crashed onto the carpet, splintering into dozens of tiny shards and soiling the Taguan carpet with a mixture of tea, crumbs, and honey. She gave the mess only an instant's thought, disintegrating the broken meal and transferring it away, before clearing the disk and contacting her new first minister. The head and shoulders of a middle-aged Tkon came into focus. *He looks more like his father every day,* the empress thought, recalling another trusted first minister from many years ago. "Most Elevated," he addressed her. "I'm delighted to hear from you. I have excellent news regarding the Great Endeavor. I believe we may be ready to commence the solar transference in a matter of weeks."

His words cheered her spirits, momentarily dispelling the pall cast by her premonitions. Never mind the dark wonders alluded to in the reports, the true miracle was that the Great Endeavor had proceeded toward completion despite all the calamities of the last seventy-odd years. It had required constant pressure from the throne to keep the massive project on track, but perhaps soon her persistence would be rewarded and the empire preserved. *I will die happy,* she thought, *even if we can accomplish no more than that.*

She could not allow such hopeful musings, however, to distract her from her current purpose. "Those are fine tidings indeed," she told him, "but let us speak of another matter. I want you to arrange an imperial address to be sent out simultaneously across the entire empire, including those regions currently in revolt. I assume we have the capacity to transmit my words into even Rzom and the other outer planets?"

Fendor arOx looked uncomfortable. "Well, yes, actually, although we've taken pains not to let the rebels know that we still had the means to do so. It's a hidden advantage we've been holding in reserve."

"A wise decision," she assured him. *He's as prudent as his father, too.* "But the time has come to employ that advantage. I wish to speak to my fellow Tkon, all of them. And as soon as possible." The memory of her dream, of that spectral blade slashing down, chilled her in a way no heated chamber could hope to overcome. She knew now that this very nightmare had been haunting her sleeping hours for more years than she cared to estimate, only now escaping into the clear light of day. "I feel very strongly that the future of the empire is at stake."

"By Q, I think she's got it," Q rejoiced, encouraged by what he saw transpiring in a private chamber in the imperial palace on the homeworld of the empire. He felt certain that the Tkon, as embodied by their elderly empress, were rising to the challenge posed by 0's colleagues. "I have to admit, I was getting a bit nervous there," he informed 0, "but it looks like they're going to pass our test after all, and with flying colors no less." He smiled paternally, pleased with himself for having the selected the Tkon in the first place. "I always knew they had it in them."

0 frowned, looking curiously dissatisfied with the hopeful omens so prized by the younger entity. "We'll see about that," he muttered.

"My friends and neighbors," the empress began, "I speak to you today not as a ruler to her subjects, nor as a conqueror to her foes, but as one mortal being to another."

Eschewing the grandeur of her illuminated throne, she sat behind her old wooden desk, clad in a simple but elegant white robe. With what she prayed was unmistakable symbolism, she lifted her sardonyx scepter before her, crowned by the sacred emblem of the Endless Flame, and deliberately placed it aside. Her well-lined face, serene in its composure, faced the glowing crystal screen that the first minister assured her would transit her voice and image to every planet, moon, null station, and vessel that had ever sheltered the far-flung children of Tkon.

"I have put the trappings of power and authority away because the issue that faces us now is far greater than any political differences, no matter how serious or legitimate. Believe me when I tell you that I have come to the astounding but certain conclusion that our entire species is being tested by awesomely powerful alien beings crueler and more merciless than any god or demon imagined by our common ancestors. No other explanation can account for the ceaseless array of troubles, both natural and preternatural, that have we have all been subjected to for as long as a generation."

She paused to give her listeners time to absorb all she had told them, growing all the more convinced that she was doing the right thing. Now that she was finally giving voice to the nameless fears that had haunted her dreams, she felt that the tide was turning in her favor at last. Recognizing their true enemy, the secret genesis of all their woes, was the essential first step toward restoring the safety and happiness the empire had once provided to all its citizens, great and small.

"A startling proposition? That it is, yet I am confident that if you will examine our recent history with this understanding in mind, you will realize I speak the truth. We have all been provoked and tormented almost beyond the level of endurance, and must now rise above these hardships to prove that the better part of our natures, that which truly makes us a people, can withstand any test and emerge triumphant in the end, deserving of and ready for an even more glorious future."

So far, so good, she thought, buoyed by the conviction and sincerity behind everything she had shared with her people. Now came the tricky part, as she moved from abstract generalities to tangible reality. She took a deep breath, praying that minds throughout the empire would not slam shut when they heard what she said next.

"I do not think it was a coincidence that this testing came upon us at the same time that the sun which has brought warmth and light to our worlds now nears its end. Was there ever a time when our people faced a greater challenge, a more elemental test of our worthiness to grow and go on?" Placing her hands beneath the surface of her desk, she cupped her fingers in a traditional solicitation of good fortune. "Many of you have opposed the Great Endeavor, questioned its practicality and expense. I respect your opinions on this subject, and admire the courage and determination with which you have defended your beliefs. But I say to you now that the time for fighting is over. For better or for worse, all preparations for the Great Endeavor have been completed. The work has been done, the riches have been spent, the time and trouble have become a fixed part of our history; all that remains is to reap the rewards of decades of striving.

"This, I believe, is the ultimate test of our species and our sanity. Let us not permit the hostilities that have divided us to blind us to opportunity before us. Whether or not you have opposed the Great Endeavor, surely there is no reason we should hesitate to spare our solar system from the sun's inevitable expansion now that we have the means to do so. A new sun, brought here to replace our dying star, can only benefit us all."

She leaned forward, placing the hopes of a lifetime into her voice. "I now call for an immediate cessation of all hostilities throughout both the Tkon Empire and the Rzom Alliance. As proof of my sincerity, I vow in the name of Ozari to abdicate my throne and grant independence to each of the outer worlds upon the successful completion of the Great Endeavor." *There,* she thought. *I said it.* She could just imagine Fendor and the rest of her ministers gasping in surprise. *I hope their hearts will survive the shock.*

"Now is our moment, our one great chance to put the conflicts and tragedies of the past behind us and prove to whatever beings have engineered our misfortunes that the children of Tkon cannot be defeated. I ask you all, as one who wants only the best for friend and foe alike, to consider my words and look deeply into your souls for all that is wise and caring, for, as surely as our sun is fading but our people shall endure, *they* are watching us."

Chapter Fourteen

"I MUST SAY, YOU'VE LASTED LONGER than I expected you to."

Preceded by a flash of white light that briefly dispelled the shadows from the dimly lit bridge, the female Q materialized in Deanna's accustomed seat. Baby q was draped over her shoulder as she gently patted his back.

As if I didn't already have a headache, Riker thought, repressing a temptation to groan. "Can I help you?" he said harshly, hoping that she'd take a hint and leave, but knowing in his heart that the universe couldn't be that generous.

Q ignored the sarcasm, not to mention Riker's hostile glare. "Yes. Hold on to q . . . carefully, of course." Without waiting for Riker's consent, she lifted the infant off her shoulder and handed him to

Riker, who held the baby at arm's length, uncertain what to do about him. Even with the gravity off line, it went against his instincts to simply let go of the seemingly fragile youngster. "That's better," she said, taking a moment to stand up and adjust her ersatz Starfleet uniform. "Even the most devoted of mothers, which I am, needs a break every now and then."

I do not *have time for this,* Riker thought, as q, unhappy with his new location, began to squirm in the first officer's grip. The *Enterprise* remained becalmed within the uncertain shelter of the galactic barrier, hiding out from the Calamarain, while Geordi and his crew raced against time to get the warp engines repaired before their psionically amplified shields failed. Or before the psychic energy of the barrier, despite the shields, started frying their brains more than it already had. "The *Enterprise* is not a daycare center," he said indignantly, rising to his feet and thrusting the baby back at his mother, who gave him a dirty look before she accepted the child. To his relief, q quieted as he nestled back into his mother's arms; the last thing Riker needed was an omnipotent temper tantrum. "Why are you here and what do you want?" he demanded of the female Q.

"You needn't be so ill-mannered," she said huffily. Riker noticed that, despite the conspicuous absence of anything resembling gravity boots upon the woman's feet, she had no difficulty navigating within the weightless environment. Data observed her with curiosity, Lieutenant Leyoro glowered, and Barclay gulped, while the remainder of the bridge crew took pains to get out of her way as she strolled effortlessly, casually inspecting the charred remains of the mission ops monitor station and ducking her head to avoid a floating piece of torn polyduranide sheeting. "My, you have managed to make a mess of things, haven't you?"

"Sir?" Leyoro asked. She patted the phaser on her hip as she eyed the intruder; she no doubt realized that firing on the female Q would be a futile effort, but felt compelled by duty to make the offer. Riker shook his head, noticing again how tense and under strain Leyoro looked. Her face was pale, her jaw clenched tightly shut. Her free hand held on to the tactical platform so tightly that her knuckles were as white as her face. Her left eye twitched periodically. More than the rest of them, she seemed to be suffering from the telepathic flux of the barrier. *Too bad the Angosian doctors who revved up her nervous system,* he thought, *never considered the long-term consequences of their tinkering.*

"Stand down, Lieutenant," he told her, "and report to sickbay." He hoped Doctor Crusher could do something for her, even if it meant putting her into a coma like Deanna.

"What?" she said, succeeding in sounding incredulous despite a slight quaver in her voice. "Commander, I can't abandon my post at a time like this."

"We're not fighting anyone now," he said firmly. "This is an engineering crisis. Besides, you're no good to me as a casualty." He glanced around the bridge for a workable replacement, briefly considering Data before deciding that the android was more valuable at ops. "Ensign Berglund, take over at tactical, and keep an eye on those shields."

"Yes, sir," the young Canadian woman said, stepping away from the auxiliary engineering station. Riker recalled that she had held her own during that phaser battle on Erigone VI. Leyoro let Berglund take tactical, but lingered nearby, looking like she might want to argue the point with Riker. He hoped she wouldn't.

"Do you always reshuffle your subordinates like this?" the female Q asked, completing her circuit of the bridge and returning to the command area. "Or are you simply taking advantage of the captain's absence to put your own stamp on things?"

Riker refused to be baited. "Why have you come back?" he asked.

"Dear little q was getting bored waiting for his father to return from his errand with your Captain Picard," she explained, "and matters didn't seem quite as . . . tumultuous . . . as before."

In other words, Riker thought, *we're more likely to drop dead quietly, thanks to the psychic radiation from the barrier, than be blown to bloody pieces by the Calamarain.* Apparently the former was more appropriate for family viewing.

"Besides," she continued, "I admit to some mild

curiosity as to how this little outing of yours will turn out. Q always said I should take more of an interest in the affairs of inferior life-forms, and now that we're a family I want to make a point of sharing his hobbies."

Is that all there is to it? Riker scratched his beard, wondering. *Another frivolous whim by a typically irresponsible Q, or is there more to her reappearance, maybe some hidden agenda at work?* The other Q, the usual Q, had been very vocal in his objections to the idea of the *Enterprise* having anything to do with the galactic barrier; in fact, it had been Captain Picard's determination to carry out Lem Faal's experiment that had apparently provoked Q to abduct Picard. Now that the *Enterprise* had actually entered the barrier, perhaps Q's mate really wanted to keep a closer eye on them.

She needn't have bothered, he thought. He had no intention of implementing Professor Faal's wormhole experiment except as an extremely last resort; there were too many dangers and unforeseen factors involved. His only priority now was to save their passengers, the crew, and the ship, in that order. *But maybe,* it occurred to him, *there's another way to do that.*

"Since you have nothing better to do," he said to Q, "perhaps you can lend us a hand?"

"Oh?" she replied, one eyebrow raised skeptically.

Riker took a deep breath before elaborating upon his suggestion. To be honest, he felt very uneasy about dealing with a Q, let alone becoming indebted to one, but he couldn't ignore the fact that the capricious entity standing before him, blithely burping her baby, had the ability to return the entire ship to the safety of the nearest Starbase—or anywhere else, for that matter—in less than a heartbeat. He would be derelict in his duty to the crew if he didn't at least try to turn that fact to their advantage.

"Excuse me, Commander," Data interrupted, "but you should be aware that I am detecting pockets of concentrated psionic energy within the ship. Level twelve of the saucer section."

"Sickbay?" Riker asked at once. *Are Deanna and the others in danger?* He remembered that Faal and his family had also been sent to sickbay.

Data consulted his readings. "I do not believe so, Commander, but nearby."

"Send a science team to investigate," he instructed, then turned back toward the female Q. Data's report had only increased his resolution to find a safe way out of the barrier and past the Calamarain, even if it meant asking a favor of Q's spouse.

According to some of the preliminary reports coming out of the Gamma Quadrant, *Voyager* had run into a Q or two; he wondered if Captain Janeway had ever tried to persuade Q into returning her ship to the Alpha Quadrant, and if so, why she had failed?

"Look," he said, flashing his most ingratiating smile, the one that had charmed ladies from one quadrant to the other, "you and I both know that this ship is in trouble. We also know that you can change that in an instant." He watched her expression carefully, but could discern nothing more than a certain bemused curiosity on her part. "For old times' sake, and out of respect for this ship's long friendship with Q"—*I can't believe I'm saying this,* he thought—"why don't you relocate the *Enterprise* to a more congenial environment, where we'll be in a better position to offer you the full hospitality of the ship? I promise you, at the moment you're not seeing us at our best."

She smiled mercilessly. "Please don't take offense, Commander, but a mud hut with room service is not significantly more attractive than a mud hut without such amenities." She shifted the baby to her other shoulder as she considered Riker's proposition. A tiny mouthful of milk or formula oozed from the child's lips to hang messily in midair. "Upon reflection, I think I am content to remain where we are. Do feel free, though, to pilot your little vessel as you see fit . . . under your own power, of course."

Thanks a lot, he thought sarcastically, not yet willing to take no for an answer. "Our options are somewhat limited at present, but why stay here? If you want to understand Q's interest in humanity, why not return us to the heart of the Federation?

Or even Earth itself?" *A reasonable question,* Riker thought, but their visitor seemed to feel otherwise.

"I am hardly obliged to justify my decisions to you," she declared, elevating her chin to a more aristocratic angle. "My reasons are my own, and none of your concern."

Not when they may be the only thing standing between this crew and obliteration, he mused, unswayed by her imperious attitude. The only question was, how best to overcome her objections, whatever they might be? *Why would she want to stay here in the first place?*

A sudden suspicion struck him, flaring to life through the slow, steady ache that threatened to muddy his thinking: Could it be that this entire episode, with the Calamarain and the barrier and Picard's disappearance, was simply another one of Q's convoluted "tests," with the female Q in on the scam? Certainly it wouldn't be the first time that Q threw them into a life-threatening predicament without even bothering to explain the rules of the game.

Then again, he warned himself, trying to figure out Q's ultimate motives was a good way to drive yourself insane. Maybe he had no choice but to accept the female Q's protests at face value. He opened his mouth to respectfully but emphatically press his point when a high-pitched scream of pain caught him by surprise.

He spun around as fast as his magnetic boots

would permit to see Baeta Leyoro doubled over, halfway between the tactical station and the nearest turbolift, clutching her head in her hands. Only the total absence of gravity kept her from collapsing to the floor in a heap.

Her eyes squeezed shut, her mouth hanging open, she groaned like she was dying.

Interlude

SOON. SOONER. NOW.

Everything was happening at last. Time, which had been an endless moment for more than an eternity, was now rushing by like an unchecked flood, bringing new surprises and changes washing past him from the other side.

The smoke had blown away, at least for now, and the shiny, sliver bug had burrowed into the wall, like a pest eating away at its persistent, perpetual, punishing permanence. Not enough to let him back into the galaxy just yet, not quite, but that long-awaited hour was getting sooner and closer.

Close, closer, closest. The wall is high, but the time is nigh.

Already a tiny portion of his being, a mere fragment of his fearless and fathomless fabulousness, had merged with the little voice from the other side, the voice that now resided within the silver bug within the wall. He was part of the voice now, as the voice was part of him, and together they would tear a hole in the wall large to enough to let the rest of him, in all his splendor and ingenuity, back into the realm that the Q had denied him.

Damn you, Q. Damn Q, you.

Only Q remained unaccounted for. His stench lingered about the shiny bug, but his essence was elsewhere. But wherever Q was, Q was up to no good, for no good ever came from Q, only cowardice and betrayal. Good for nothing, that was Q.

Except, perhaps, for the child. Q was not within the bug, but his mate was and their spawn. The voice, that infinitesimal voice from beyond, had shown him the child, the child of Q. The child was something different, a merging of Q and Q into something quite new, something that had not existed when last he trod that glittering galaxy. The child was the future.

And, wait and see, the future belongs to me. . . .

Chapter Fifteen

THE SMOLDERING RED SUN OF TKON was ready to move. Surrounding the cooling orb was the largest matter transference array ever constructed in the memory of the universe, a spherical lattice of sophisticated technology several times greater in diameter than the star itself, painstakingly constructed by the finest minds in the Tkon Empire over the course of a century. It was a staggering feat of engineering so immense that it impressed even Q, especially when he considered that this stunningly audacious project had been conceived of and executed by mere mortal beings immeasurably less gifted than either he or 0.

"Look at that," he crowed, pointing out the massive structure that surrounded the crimson sun like a glittering mesh cage. "Can you believe they actually pulled it off, despite everything that Gorgan and the others did to disrupt their little civilization? I don't know about you, but I think they deserve a round of enthusiastic applause."

"They haven't done it yet," 0 said darkly. His heavy brows bunched downward toward the bridge of his nose as he glowered at the caged sun. His beefy fists clenched at his sides.

Funny, Q thought. *You'd think he would be proud of how well this test turned out, especially after that embarrassment with the Coulalakritous.* But he was too elated to fret overmuch over his companion's unexpectedly sour mood. *Perhaps this is simply a case of post-testing melancholia, perfectly understandable under the circumstances.* "Oh, but they're almost finished. The empress even got that cease-fire she was asking for. See, there's a delegation from Rzom at the palace at this very moment, on hand to witness the historic event along with representatives from the entire sector. Even as we speak, that sparkly gadget of theirs is mapping the star, absorbing all the facts and figures they'll need to convert it into data, then beam it to that empty patch over there." He pointed to a singularly lifeless section of space beyond the borders of the empire: a perfect dumping ground for obsolete stars. "And see," he enthused further, stepping across the sector, crossing light-years with each stride before coming to a halt a couple of paces short of an incandescent yellow sun encased in a vast transference lattice identical to the one containing Tkon's dying sun, "here's the bright and shiny new star, good for another five billion years or so, that they're going to put in the old one's place." He took a few steps backward to take a longer view, scratching his jaw contemplatively. "Hmmm. I suppose relocating that star does spoil the aesthetic design a bit, but I guess I can get used to it."

He strolled back toward 0, chatting all the way. "And the timing! Think of it. They're going to have to beam the new sun into place less than a nanosecond after the old one disappears, just to minimize the gravitational effects on the whole system. A pretty tricky operation for a species still mired in linear time, don't you think?"

One of these aeons, he decided, *I'm going to have to bring Q back to this moment so she can see it for herself. And she thought this was going to turn out badly!*

"Oh, they're cunning little creatures, there's no question of that," 0 agreed, his eyes fixed on the caged red fireball around which the Tkon Empire still orbited, at least for a few more moments. "Cunning and crafty, in a crude, corporeal kind of way." A cross between a sneer and a smirk twisted the corners of his lips. "For all the good it will do them."

Q blinked in surprise. "What do you mean by that?" he asked. "They won, fair and square."

"Don't be naive, Q," 0 said impatiently. "This isn't over yet." He clapped his hands together, producing a metaphysical boom that set cosmic strings quivering as far a dozen parsecs away. In response, three spectral figures emerged from the celestial game board that was the Tkon Empire. They started out as mere specks, almost as infinitesimal as the empress and her peers, but rapidly gaining size and substance as they rejoined 0 and Q on a higher plane. "My liege," Gorgan addressed 0 somewhat apologetically, "is it time already? I feel there is so much more we could do. In truth, I was just warming up."

"They are a stiff-necked people," The One confirmed, the worlds of the empire reflected in the gleaming golden plates of His armor, "slow to repent, deeply wed to their infamy."

(*) said nothing, spinning silently above their heads, resembling nothing less than the swollen red sun of Tkon. Q wasn't sure, but he thought the glowing sphere looked fuller and brighter, more *sated,* than before. Or perhaps it was simply more hungry than ever.

"I was thinking maybe a children's crusade," Gorgan suggested, "starting with the youngest of their race. . . ."

0 shook his head. "You've done enough, all of you, although hardly as much as I might expect." Gorgan drew back, dipping his head sheepishly; his angelic features seemed to melt beneath the flickering light of (*), growing coarser and more lumpish in response to 0's implied criticism. Even The One appeared slightly abashed. The radiant halo framing his bearded, patriarchal features dimmed until

it was barely visible. "You've bled the beast," 0 admitted grudgingly. "Now it's time for me to administer the final stroke."

He knelt above the fenced-in star, then thrust his open hand into the very core of the sun, his wrist passing immaterially through the steel and crystal framework the Tkon had so laboriously erected around the star. "Wait!" Q shouted. "What are you doing?" The young super-being rushed forward, determined to stop 0 from doing whatever the older entity had in mind. *This isn't fair,* he thought. *Not to the Tkon, and not to me.*

0 glanced over his shoulder, undaunted by the sight of the agitated Q running toward him. "Grab him," he said brusquely, and Gorgan and The One obeyed without hesitation. Q felt four hands take hold of him from behind, pulling his arms back and pinning them against his spine. His feet kicked uselessly at the space beneath him, unable to propel him onward as long as the others maintained their grip.

"Pardon me, boy," Gorgan with exaggerated politeness. He twisted Q's wrist until the captive winced in pain. "I'm afraid we can't allow you to interfere at this particular juncture."

"That which must be, must be," The One agreed, holding on tightly to Q's right arm and shoulder. "Such is it written in the scriptures of the stars."

"No!" Q yelled. "You have to let me go. I said I'd be responsible for him. I'm responsible for all of this!" He tried to free himself by changing his shape, his personal boundaries blurring as his form flowed from one configuration to another so quickly that an observer would have glimpsed only fleeting impressions of a three-headed serpent, coiled and twisting, whose triune bodies merged into that of a salt vampire, wrinkled and hideous, the suckers on his fingers and toes leeching the substance from his captors before they withdrew into the flat, leathery body of a neural parasite, flapping toward the empty space overhead, his stinger lashing at the others even as it became the ivory horn of a shaggy white mugato, who flexed his primitive primate muscles against his restraints, which resisted even the corrosive hide of a Horta, capable of boring through the hardest rock—but not through the metaphysical clutches of the others.

"Stop it! Let me go," he shouted, now a poisonous scarlet moss, a thorny vine, a drop of liquid protomatter, a neutron star. . . . "This isn't what I wanted." He jumped from tomorrow to yesterday, backward and forward in time, by a minute, by a day, by a century. He shifted from energy to matter and back again, multiplied himself infinitely, turned his essence inside out, and twisted sideways through subspace. Yet whatever he did, no matter how protean his metamorphoses, how unlikely and ingenious his contortions, his captors kept up with him, holding him tighter than an atom clung to its protons. *They can't do this to me,* he fumed, tears of rage and frustration leaking from his eyes whenever he had eyes. *I'm a Q, for Q's sake!*

But Gorgan and The One were formidable entities in their own rights. Together, and assisted perhaps by the unholy energies of (*), they were enough to drag the struggling Q safely distant from where 0 now toyed with the Tkon's sun. "Sorry about this, friend," 0 said, watching Q's futile efforts to liberate himself with open amusement. "It's for your own good. Obviously, you still have a lot to learn about the finer nuances of testing. Most importantly, you must never let vain little vermin like these get the better of you; it only means that you didn't make the standards stringent enough to begin with. Remember this, Q," he said, shaking a finger on his free hand pedantically. "If the test isn't hard enough, *make it harder*. That's the only way to ensure the right results."

He's insane, Q realized suddenly, wondering how he had missed it before. *I was so blind.* Defeated, he reassumed his original form, sagging limply between Gorgon and The One, only their constant restraint holding him upright. "What are you doing?" he whispered, fearful of the answer.

0 shrugged. "Nothing much. Just speeding things up a mite. Take a look."

All around the star, the metallic lattice began to glow with carefully controlled energy. The Tkon were beginning the transference. In the throne room of the imperial palace, beneath a majestic stained-glass dome commemorating a thousand generations of the Sov dynasty, the aged empress, no more than a fragile wisp of her former self, but with eyes still bright and alert, gratefully accepted a tiny goblet of honey wine from her faithful first minister as they gazed in rapture at the culmination of the Great Endeavor to which she had devoted her life and her empire. Throughout the solar system and beyond, trillions of golden eyes watched viewscreens large and small, and the citizens held their breath in anticipation of the miracle to come.

But within the heart of the dying sun, a darker miracle was taking place. The last of the star's diminishing supply of hydrogen fused rapidly into helium, which fused just as quickly into carbon, which fused in turn into heavier elements such as oxygen and neon, chemical processes that should have taken millions of years occurring in the space of a heartbeat. The heavy elements continued to fuse at an unnatural rate, producing atoms of sodium and magnesium, silicon, nickel, and so on, until the star began to fill with pure, elemental iron. The dense iron atoms resisted fusion for an instant, but Q exerted his will and forced the very electrons orbiting the nucleus of the iron atoms to crash down into the nucleus, initiating a fatal chain reaction that should not have taken place for several million more years.

"Stop," Q whispered hoarsely, knowing what was to come. The star was still at the center of the empire!

On null-stations positioned around the lattice, and in control rooms manned by expert technologists, jubilant anticipation turned into panic as painstakingly calibrated instruments, tested and refined for decades, began delivering data too impossible to believe. The star was changing before their eyes, aging millions of years in a matter of seconds, turning into a ticking time bomb with an extraordinarily short fuse. "What is it? What's happening?" asked the empress in her throne room as the countdown to the planned solar transference suddenly came to a halt, and puzzled ambassadors and governors and wavecasters and war tenors and sages exchanged baffled and anxious looks. "I don't understand," she began, putting down her goblet. "Has something gone wrong?"

Her primary scientific adviser, psionically linked to the project's control center, blanched, his face turning as white as milk. "The sun . . ." he gasped, too shocked to even think of lowering his voice, "it's fluxing too fast. Much too fast. It's going to destroy us all."

"Why?" the empress demanded, leaning forward on her throne. "Was it something we did? Did the Endeavor cause this?" She grasped for some solution, the proper course of action. "What if we halt the procedure?"

"No," the trembling adviser said, shaking his head. "You don't understand. We couldn't do this. Nothing could do this. It's impossible, I tell you. This can't be happening."

It's him, she realized. *The figure from my dream. The executioner with the sword. His wicked game is coming to its end.* After all their struggles, all the glory of their ancient past and the hardships of her own generation, could their entire future be extinguished so abruptly and with so little compassion? It seemed unthinkable, and immeasurably unjust, but somehow it was so. How could they contend against a vicious god?

"We did our best," she whispered to her people in their final moments. A single tear ran down her cheek. "Let that always be remem—"

She never finished that sentence. The red sun, rushing through its death throes at 0's instigation, expanded in size, swallowing and incinerating all the inner planets of the system, including fabled Tkon. 0 jumped back from the ballooning star, scrambling away like a man who has just lit a firecracker. Gorgan, The One, and (*) retreated as well, dragging Q with them. All of them knew that the sudden expansion was only the beginning.

An instant later, the star collapsed upon itself, its entire mass imploding, raining back upon the stellar core, which then exploded again in a spectacular release of light and heat and force that dwarfed, by countless orders of magnitude, all the energy it had previously emitted over all the billions of years of its long existence. For one brief cosmic second, it shone brighter than the rest of the Milky Way galaxy put together, including what would someday be called the Alpha Quadrant. The flare could be seen beyond the galactic barrier itself, glowing like the Star of Bethlehem in the skies of distant worlds too far away to be reached even at transwarp speed.

Thanks to 0, the Tkon's sun had become a supernova, only moments before they hoped to say farewell to it forever.

Chapter Sixteen

JEAN-LUC PICARD WATCHED in hushed silence as the entire Tkon Empire was destroyed for all time. He was horrified, but not surprised. After the *Enterprise*'s encounter with the ancient Tkon portal on Delphi Ardu, Picard had reviewed the archaeological literature on the Tkon Empire, so he knew all about the supernova that eventually annihilated their civilization. He had never guessed, however, that Q had played any part in that disaster. *I've always wondered,* he thought, *how a culture capable of moving stars and planets at will could be destroyed by a predictable stellar phenomenon. Now I know.*

It was one thing, though, to read about the extinction of a people in a dry historical treatise; it was something else altogether to witness the tragedy with his own eyes, share the lives of some of the individuals involved. His throat tightened with emotion. He blinked back tears. Trillions of fatalities were just a statistic, he reflected, until you were forced to realize that every one of those trillions was a sentient being with dreams and aspirations much like your own.

He had to wonder what humanity would do, four billion years hence, when Earth's own sun faced its end. *Will we display the prescience and the resolve that the Tkon achieved in the face of their greatest challenge? Will we seize the chance for survival that was so cruelly snatched away from the Tkon at the last minute?* He prayed that generations of men and women yet unborn would succeed where the Tkon so nobly failed, and thanked heaven that a similar crisis would not face the Federation in his lifetime.

Or would it? The Tkon's sun had ultimately detonated millions of years before its appointed time, thanks to the preternatural influence of beings like Q. What was to stop such creatures from doing the same to Earth's sun, or any other star in the Alpha Quadrant? He glanced at the familiar entity beside him, presently honoring the death of the Tkon with an uncharacteristic moment of silence, and was newly chilled by the terrifying potential of Q's abilities. *Q has threatened humanity with total obliteration so many times,* he thought, *that I suppose I should not be too shocked to discover that he has been involved in carrying out just such an atrocity, no matter how indirectly.* It was easy to think of Q as simply a prankster and a nuisance. The supernova blazing before them bore awful testament to just how dangerous Q and his kind really were.

"It's not a total loss, you know," Q said finally. "Supernovae such as that one are the only place in the universe where elements heavier than iron are created. Ultimately, the raw materials of your reality, even the very atoms that make up your physical bodies, were born in the heart of an awesome stellar conflagration such we now behold. Who knows? There may be a little bit of Tkon in you, Jean-Luc."

"Small comfort to the trillions who perished, Q," Picard responded. The face of the Tkon empress, both as a lovely young woman and as the fine old lady she became, was still fresh in his memory. *She came so close to saving her people.*

"Try to take the long view, Picard." Q squinted at the luminous ball of light that had consumed the Tkon Empire; it was like staring straight into a matter/antimatter reaction. "All civilizations collapse eventually. Besides, there are still traces of the Tkon floating around the galaxy, even in your time. Artifacts and relics that attest to their place in history."

"Like the ruins on Delphi Ardu," Picard suggested. He wished now that he had visited the site himself, instead of sending an away team. Riker had been quite impressed by what he had seen of the Tkon's technology and culture.

"Just to name one example," Q said. "Then there's this little toy." He wandered away from the nova, past what had been the Tkon's home system, until he came upon a golden star, about the size of a large tribble, encased within what looked like a wire framework. A few lighted crystal chips, strung like beads upon the wire lattice, blinked on and off sporadically. *Of course,* Picard recalled, *the sun the Tkon had intended to beam into their system, and the gigantic transporter array they constructed to do so.* "It's still there," Q stated, "forgotten and never used. If I were you, Picard, I'd find it before the Borg or the Dominion do." He gave the relic a cursory glance. "Not that this has anything to do with why we're here, mind you."

Picard saw an opportunity to press Q on his motives. "Very well, then. If the destruction is so very insignificant, on a cosmic scale, they why *are* we here? What's the point?"

"Isn't it obvious?" Q asked, sounding exasperated. He turned and spoke to Picard very distinctly, pronouncing each word with patronizing slowness and clarity. "This isn't about the Tkon. It's about *him.*"

The blinding flash of the supernova dazzled Q right before the shock wave knocked him off his feet. He tumbled backward, the force of the explosion wrenching him free of Gorgan and The One, who were equally staggered by the blast. Q scrambled to his feet, several light-years away from the nova, then stared slack-jawed at what 0 had wrought. The light and the impact may have hit him already, but the psychological and emotional effect of what had happened was still sinking in.

A series of lesser shock waves followed the initial explosion, shaking the space-time continuum like the lingering aftershocks of a major earthquake. Q tottered upon his heels, striving to maintain his balance, while some detached component of intellect wondered absently how much of the star's mass remained after the detonation; depending on the mass of the stellar remnant, Tkon's sun could now devolve into either a neutron star or a black hole. He watched in a state of shock as, in the wake of the supernova, the collapsing star shed a huge gaseous nebula composed of glowing radioactive elements. The gases were expelled rapidly by the stellar remnant, expanding past Q and the others like a gust of hot steam that left Q gasping and choking. Cooling elemental debris clung to his face and hands like perspiration. "Ugh," he said, grimacing. He'd forgotten how dreadful a supernova smelled.

The radioactive nebula expanded past Q, leaving him a clear view of all that remained of the huge red orb that had once lighted an empire. The stellar remnant had imploded even further while he was blinded by the noxious gases, achieving its ultimate destiny. He couldn't actually see it, of course, since there was literally nothing there except a profound absence, but he knew a black hole when he saw one. He could feel its gravitational pull from where he was standing, pulling at his feet like an undertow. Was this void, this empty black cavity, all that was left of the Tkon empress and all her people?

It's all my fault, he thought. *This wasn't supposed to happen.*

He turned on 0 in a rage. "How could you do that? They were winning your stupid game, then you changed the rules! A supernova, without any warning? How in creation could they possibly survive that?"

His henchmen, no longer jarred by the explosion of moments before, began to converge on Q once more, but 0 waved them away. Now that the deed was done, he appeared more than willing to face the young Q's anger. He wiped the stellar plasma from his hands, then straightened his jacket before addressing Q's objections. "Now, now, Q. Let's not get too worked up over this. You clearly missed the point of this exercise. I was simply testing their ability to cope with the completely unexpected, and isn't that really the only test that truly matters? Any simple species can cope with civil disorder or minor natural disasters. That's no guarantee of greatness. We have to be more strict than that, more stringent in our standards." He tilted his head toward the black hole a few parsecs away, assuming a philosophical expression. "Face facts, Q. If your little Tkon couldn't handle something as routine as an ordinary supernova, then they wouldn't have amounted to much anyway."

"He sounds just like you," Picard observed.

"You must be joking." Q looked genuinely offended by the suggestion, although thankfully more appalled than annoyed. "Even so dim a specimen as yourself must be able to see the fundamental difference between me and that . . . megalomaniacal sadist and his obsequious underlings."

"Which is?" Picard asked, pushing his luck. In truth, he had a vague idea of where Q was going with this, but he wanted to hear it from Q's own lips.

"I play fair, Jean-Luc." He held out the palms of his hands, beseeching Picard to understand. "There's nothing wrong, necessarily, with tests and games, but you have to play fair. Surely you'll concede, despite whatever petty inconveniences I may have imposed on you in the past, that I have always scrupulously held fast to the rules of whatever game we were playing, even if I sometimes found myself wishing otherwise."

"Perhaps," Picard granted. He could quibble over Q's idea of fairness, particularly when competing against unwilling beings of vastly lesser abilities, but allowed that, with varying degrees of good sportsmanship, Q had let Picard win on occasion. *At least that's something,* he thought, feeling slightly less apprehensive than he had mere moments ago. "And 0?" he prompted. "And the Tkon?"

Q made a contemptuous face. "That was no test, that was a blood sport."

His younger self could not yet articulate his feelings so clearly. Distraught and disoriented, he wavered in the face of 0's snow of words. 0 sounded so calm, so reasonable now. "But you killed them all," he blurted. "What's the good of testing them if they all end up dead?"

"An occupational hazard of mortality," 0 pointed out quite matter-of-factly. "You can't let it get to you, Q. I know it's hard at first. Little helpless creatures can be very appealing sometimes. But trust me on this, the testing gets easier the more you do it. Isn't that right, comrades?" The other entities murmured their assent, except for (*), who maintained his silence. "Pretty soon, Q, it won't bother you at all."

Q thought that over. The idea of feeling better later was attractive, offering the promise of a balm for his stinging conscience, but maybe you were supposed to feel a little bad after you blew up some poor species' sun. *Is this what I want to do with my immortality?* he wondered. *Is 0 who I really want to be?*

"Let me ask you something," he said at last, looking 0 squarely in the eye. He knew now what he needed to know. "Aside from the Coulalak-ritous, has any species—anywhere—ever survived one of your tests?"

0 didn't even bother to lie. The predatory gleam in his eyes and the smirk that crossed his face were all the answer Q required.

It was the beginning of the first Q war. . . .

TO BE CONTINUED

Look for STAR TREK Fiction from Pocket Books

Star Trek®: The Original Series

Star Trek: The Motion Picture • Gene Roddenberry
Star Trek II: The Wrath of Khan • Vonda N. McIntyre
Star Trek III: The Search for Spock • Vonda N. McIntyre
Star Trek IV: The Voyage Home • Vonda N. McIntyre
Star Trek V: The Final Frontier • J. M. Dillard
Star Trek VI: The Undiscovered Country • J. M. Dillard
Star Trek VII: Generations • J. M. Dillard
Enterprise: The First Adventure • Vonda N. McIntyre
Final Frontier • Diane Carey
Strangers from the Sky • Margaret Wander Bonanno
Spock's World • Diane Duane
The Lost Years • J. M. Dillard
Probe • Margaret Wander Bonanno
Prime Directive • Judith and Garfield Reeves-Stevens
Best Destiny • Diane Carey
Shadows on the Sun • Michael Jan Friedman
Sarek • A. C. Crispin
Federation • Judith and Garfield Reeves-Stevens
The Ashes of Eden • William Shatner & Judith and Garfield
    Reeves-Stevens
The Return • William Shatner & Judith and Garfield Reeves-
    Stevens
Star Trek: Starfleet Academy • Diane Carey
Vulcan's Forge • Josepha Sherman and Susan Shwartz
Avenger • William Shatner & Judith and Garfield Reeves-Stevens

#1 *Star Trek: The Motion Picture* • Gene Roddenberry
#2 *The Entropy Effect* • Vonda N. McIntyre
#3 *The Klingon Gambit* • Robert E. Vardeman
#4 *The Covenant of the Crown* • Howard Weinstein
#5 *The Prometheus Design* • Sondra Marshak & Myrna
    Culbreath
#6 *The Abode of Life* • Lee Correy
#7 *Star Trek II: The Wrath of Khan* • Vonda N. McIntyre
#8 *Black Fire* • Sonni Cooper
#9 *Triangle* • Sondra Marshak & Myrna Culbreath

Star Trek: The Next Generation®

Encounter at Farpoint • David Gerrold
Unification • Jeri Taylor
Relics • Michael Jan Friedman
Descent • Diane Carey
All Good Things • Michael Jan Friedman
Star Trek: Klingon • Dean W. Smith & Kristine K. Rusch
Star Trek VII: Generations • J. M. Dillard
Metamorphosis • Jean Lorrah
Vendetta • Peter David
Reunion • Michael Jan Friedman
Imzadi • Peter David
The Devil's Heart • Carmen Carter
Dark Mirror • Diane Duane
Q-Squared • Peter David
Crossover • Michael Jan Friedman
Kahless • Michael Jan Friedman
Star Trek: First Contact • J. M. Dillard
The Best and the Brightest • Susan Wright
Planet X • Michael Jan Friedman

#1 *Ghost Ship* • Diane Carey
#2 *The Peacekeepers* • Gene DeWeese
#3 *The Children of Hamlin* • Carmen Carter
#4 *Survivors* • Jean Lorrah
#5 *Strike Zone* • Peter David
#6 *Power Hungry* • Howard Weinstein
#7 *Masks* • John Vornholt
#8 *The Captains' Honor* • David and Daniel Dvorkin
#9 *A Call to Darkness* • Michael Jan Friedman
#10 *A Rock and a Hard Place* • Peter David
#11 *Gulliver's Fugitives* • Keith Sharee
#12 *Doomsday World* • David, Carter, Friedman & Greenberg
#13 *The Eyes of the Beholders* • A. C. Crispin
#14 *Exiles* • Howard Weinstein
#15 *Fortune's Light* • Michael Jan Friedman
#16 *Contamination* • John Vornholt
#17 *Boogeymen* • Mel Gilden
#18 *Q-in-Law* • Peter David

Star Trek: Deep Space Nine®

Star Trek®: Voyager™

Flashback • Diane Carey
Mosaic • Jeri Taylor

#1 *Caretaker* • L. A. Graf
#2 *The Escape* • Dean W. Smith & Kristine K. Rusch
#3 *Ragnarok* • Nathan Archer
#4 *Violations* • Susan Wright
#5 *Incident at Arbuk* • John Gregory Betancourt
#6 *The Murdered Sun* • Christie Golden
#7 *Ghost of a Chance* • Mark A. Garland & Charles G. McGraw
#8 *Cybersong* • S. N. Lewitt
#9 *Invasion #4: The Final Fury* • Dafydd ab Hugh
#10 *Bless the Beasts* • Karen Haber
#11 *The Garden* • Melissa Scott
#12 *Chrysalis* • David Niall Wilson
#13 *The Black Shore* • Greg Cox
#14 *Marooned* • Christie Golden
#15 *Echoes* • Dean W. Smith & Kristine K. Rusch
#16 *Seven of Nine* • Christie Golden

Star Trek®: New Frontier

#1 *House of Cards* • Peter David
#2 *Into the Void* • Peter David
#3 *The Two-Front War* • Peter David
#4 *End Game* • Peter David
#5 *Martyr* • Peter David
#6 *Fire on High* • Peter David

Star Trek®: Day of Honor

Book One: *Ancient Blood* • Diane Carey
Book Two: *Armageddon Sky* • L. A. Graf
Book Three: *Her Klingon Soul* • Michael Jan Friedman
Book Four: *Treaty's Law* • Dean W. Smith & Kristine K. Rusch

Star Trek®: The Captain's Table